The Next Dragon

"A Chicago Story"

Noah B. Shaw

Introduction

I hope that this forward finds everyone reading it in good spirits. I actually never thought about writing an introduction before, but as I put the final touches on what will be my first published novel, I decided that in the spirit of making it as legitimate as possible, I better not cut any corners.

As I am writing this, I am sitting in the main lobby of the Atlanta Hartsfield International Airport, reading "Rules to Rule By" a book written by the fictional character Ari Gold from the spectacular HBO series "Entourage." Ari was my alter ego for a while as I was making my way up the ranks in the music business as an artist manager and songwriter.

I watched every episode of Entourage in awe of how Ari handled his business and kept moving forward no matter what obstacle stood before him. Then recently I found out that there was a book by him, and I immediately went to Amazon to order my copy. I was blown away to find out that my hero was based on a real guy in Hollywood named Ari Manuel.

Around 2011, I came across this gem of a show and was instantly drawn to the character. He was calculating, ruthless and had a laser focus and a craziness that reminded me of myself in a lot of ways. At the time I was working in Sandy Springs, GA for a fortune 500 credit card processing company in their mailroom.

I was hired as a temp, and a year later, I was the supervisor. I turned that Mailroom/Copy Center into my own personal business office. I had a computer, a color copier, a telephone, a UPS shipping account monitored by me, a legal department on the 10th floor and an IT department on the 3rd. I would have made Ari proud. Who I learned, also got his start in the mailroom.

That wasn't the only thing that I had in common with my idol, upon reading his book, what really blew me away, was when I learned he had grown up in Chicago. When my parents separated, my mother moved to Rogers Park, which is on the Northside of Chicago, not too far from where Ari was raised.

I stayed with my mother up until I was 8 years old and then I moved back with my father on the SouthSide of Chicago. I eventually grew up and st arted hanging out in the streets. I did all the Gangbanging and drug dealing like everyone else around me, but I wasn't completely all the way 100 with it like some of the dudes from my area, and in Chicago if you're all the way in, you might as well pick a safer way to move up in the world.

I knew early on that my way out wouldn't be living out my Nino Brown fantasies, so I figured the best way for me was doing something creative, since sports was just about as unrealistic as starting the CMB and taking over The Carter. I developed my passion for music.

Lyrically, I was a monster and still am to this day, as I have now parlayed my rapping skills into songwriting. My intelligence and business sense would eventually lead me to artist management and branding. I'm actually president of A&R right now for my mentor's indie label, but back then rapping my way through the streets of Chicago and my propensity to gang bang got me shipped off to California as a teenager.

The early nineties saw the emergence of the "Hood" films that were a step up from the black exploitation films our parents grew up watching. Ice cube had left NWA and branched out into acting, and made the iconic movie Boyz N The Hood, written and directed by my other idol and inspiration John Singleton, who was a film school graduate who grew up in Los Angeles and was about to make his debut.

John Singleton was also about to start a garden of young black creatives when he told a young O'shea Jackson that if he could write a song, then he could write a movie. The thing was, he didn't just tell that to Ice Cube, he told that shit to ALL OF US, and I received that message loud and clear.

Fast forward, the year is 2018 and the music industry has me exhausted and rethinking my line of work, well let me clarify, I didn't want to depend on the music industry to be the source of my family's financial future, so I decided I needed re examine all the tricks I had up my sleeve and one night in the middle of an infamous drinking binge, I decided to write this book.

Today my current screen writing Jedi Master Kenya Burress has inspired me to be fearless, and to go hard like pioneers before me, such as Spike Lee, Ryan Cooglar, Lena Waithe, Issa Rae, Shonda Rimes, Dainesse Jackson, Courtney Kemp, Tyler Perry and Curtis "50 cent" Jackson, Hype Williams, Judd Apatow, Director X, Alex Tse, Will Smith, Kiki Swinson, Sister Souljah, S.E Hinton, Sophia Stewart

This work is my contribution

Acknowledgments

I would like to thank my parents for their genetic contributions to my physical form, My brothers, sisters, nieces, nephews, homeboys, ex girlfriends, people who taught me, people who had patience with me, people who corrected me, people who inspired me, people that love me, people who misunderstood me, people who listened to me, people who respect me, people who let me sleep on they couch, people who slept on my couch, people who showed me love, people who showed me music, people who showed me books, people who showed me mercy, people that showed me who they were, people who showed me their heart, people who showed their mind, people that gave me food, people that gave me their time, people who push positivity, people who share creativity, I Love you all -

Table of Contents

1.

The City

"Chicago has always been an unsung breeding ground for legends…" - Author

The sun was setting on a warm July night on the Southside of Chicago. The sky was bright orange with a touch of red, as if the city somehow knew that there would be a lot of blood shed later that night. The city itself had a rich history, from the fire that decimated its landscape in 1871 to the violent escapades of a notorious gangster named Al Capone during prohibition in the '20s. Not to mention, the political corruption in the mayor's office in the '80s and '90s to the inauguration of the first black president of the United States, and yes, as many of you may be thinking, the formation of some of the country's most notorious organized street gangs; Chicago had always maintained its own identity as the middle child between New York and

Los Angeles. Now, don't get me wrong, the city was also responsible for some of the greatest legends in sports, music, and entertainment—from Michael Jordan to Derrick Rose; Redd Foxx to Bernie Mac; Chaka Khan to Jennifer Hudson; and from Quincy Jones to Kanye West. You could say Chicago had always been an unsung breeding ground for legends, and in the summer of 2018, while unknown to most, another legend was born.

Ledarius was in the middle of one of the worst fights he had ever been in. He was already bleeding in several places, and he was pretty sure that he had a few broken ribs. He was still recovering from just having the wind knocked out of him and for the first time in his 16-years of life, he was beginning to doubt himself.

He went all out in his last exchange and threw all he had at the most dangerous adversary he had ever faced. Ledarius was pretty sure he had finally hurt him, that was until he saw him spit a glob of blood from his mouth, then he gave Ledarius a menacing look, and smiled. Then, like some sort of crazed super ninja, he sprung back up to his feet with one swift motion.

"Come on Ledarius, I'm 'bout to beat the bitch outta you," he said with a devious look in his eyes as he seemed to suddenly gain his strength back somehow. Ledarius knew what he had to do. It was situations like this that led to people getting killed or even worse, which for some time now in recent years had become all too common in the city that other cities had grown to refer to as Chiraq. Ledarius, who usually wasn't up on the latest slang had never called the city that, but, just like some kind of cruel joke, suddenly, gunshots rang out, and everybody froze.

Boom! Boom! Boom! Boom! Boom! Boom! Boom!

One of the interesting things about hearing gunshots in your general vicinity is the train of thought that follows immediately afterwards. Like, *was I hit? Did anyone else get hit? Was somebody about to just fall the fuck out on the ground right now, deader than a muthafucka, type shit*? Now, before we go any further, let me get you caught up on how we even got to this point in the first place.

Sixteen years ago, born on the night that hell must've frozen over because it was so cold in Chicago that the devil himself would have had to put a coat on. It was Christmas Eve, and Cynthia was coming down the alley past Hermitage when she had her first contraction. She tried to thug it out, but she had to stop for a minute and lean against somebody's garage until it passed. When that hawk began to blow again, hitting her uncovered neck and ankles, it motivated her to keep moving.

She was on her way back from picking up some money real quick to pay the light bill that arrived in the mail two weeks ago that she was just getting around to today. She finally arrived at the house, sat down, and called her friend Juanita to come pick her up and take her to the hospital.

Several hours later, Ledarius Amaru Tate was born at Cook County Medical at the weight of seven pounds and four ounces. He was an adorable baby boy with all ten fingers, toes, and a full head of hair. He grew up like most Chicago kids with snowball fights in the winter, video games and unorganized sports in the summer. Cynthia had her second child two years later, and was now constantly distracted by the arrival of his little brother DeQuan.

Ledarius spent most of his time either reading comics or watching the Syfy channel, and anything that involved spaceships and aliens would keep him occupied for hours.

Ledarius was a dreamer who would constantly fantasize about being caught in perilous adventures in lands far, far away. One night, while everyone was asleep, he got up and walked into the living room, turned on the television, and stumbled upon an old Karate movie starring a young Jet Li called The New Legend of Shaolin.

Not only did the fast-paced fight scenes thrill him to the core, but he was also moved by the relationship that the character Jet Li portrayed had with his young son, a highly skilled pint-sized martial arts expert in his own right, named Ting.

Ledarius was drawn to the strict discipline, yet gentle manner in which he chose to teach and guide his young apprentice. Ledarius was hooked from that moment on and began to train himself faithfully in front of the living room television every day. He studied every move in every martial arts film he could find after that.

Once, while DeQuan, who usually went by Quan, was away in the hospital, Ledarius had discovered the classic 1985 film "The Last Dragon," starring a young African American martial artist named Taimak. Taimak played the lead character who went by the name Bruce Leroy. He was the young handsome, mild mannered Karate student on his journey to find "The Master," and reach the final level, where he would be transformed and surrounded by a sublime light referred to as "The Glow."

Ledarius studied Bruce Leroy's every move and mannerism. He would practice for hours, honing his skills, and eventually, once he started practicing outside, the kids on the block started calling him "Jet Ledarius," and the name stuck.

Ledarius was obsessed and over time, actually managed to become pretty good himself. He saved up money from shoveling snow in the winter and cutting grass in the summer, and with the money, he found a real Dojo and that was where he met Master Yang. Ledarius was a natural, he dedicated all his time and energy to Kung Fu, so much so that he missed out on a lot of normal childhood experiences, and that caused him to not quite fit in so much with the rest of the kids in the neighborhood his age.

Quan, on the other hand had jumped off the porch early. He was intelligent but also very street smart, he always looked out for his brother even though Ledarius was older, But at this very moment, he was roasting Ledarius about what happens to pretty boys when they go to jail. Ledarius had court the next day and was ironing his outfit to get ready and go face the judge first thing in the morning.

2.

Ledarius

"There are many traps and pitfalls out here for young men like yourself to constantly fall into…" - *Judge Watkins*

L edarius was dressed in his Sunday's best and headed to the Cook County Juvenile Court. Teenagers of all ethnicities, from all over the city of Chicago were there, and all of them had one thing in common—they had all done something that had gotten them caught in the clutches of the legal system and found themselves here today at the mercy of the courts. Ledarius, who had never been in any trouble before, was right there along with them.

Judge Watkins was in her early fifties, but you could tell she still ate right and took immaculate care of herself, she came from behind her chambers and sat down, she spoke in a soft tone and with a wave of her hand, she told the courtroom to be seated.

Cynthia and Ledarius sat in the third row from the front, waiting for his case to be called. Judge Watkins pulled her folders in front of her, drank from a silver coffee container, looked through the folders on her desk for a moment and then she called her first case.

"Demarcus Andrews!" she yelled out as she looked down over her glasses and flipped through a few sheets of paper on her desk. A tall, slender kid in an oversized white T-shirt and a pair of baggy jeans started approaching the bench. Demarcus must've forgotten to put on his belt this morning because he kept needing to pull his pants up as he walked like a penguin up to the podium.

"Mister Andrews?" Judge Watkins said, using her inquisitive voice. "It says here that you were caught with two pounds of marijuana in a duffle bag in the trunk of your grandmother's car." She looked up again from her paperwork and glanced at the nervous teen as he pulled up his pants and then reached to tie his dreadlocks back before he spoke.

He leaned down towards the tiny microphone and said, "For real?" as if he didn't know what she was talking about. Some of the people in the courtroom let out a few giggles underneath their breath. "Yes, Mister Andrews, for real," she responded in a stern voice and gave him a quick look of confusion as a few more people began to giggle underneath their breath.

Ledarius sat behind a girl who was there because her boyfriend was incarcerated for doing his part in a botched robbery and got jammed up; he was there to be sentenced. The girlfriend had a young daughter resting her head on her mother's shoulders and was facing Ledarius, blankly staring at him the way annoying little kids do until you have to start making faces at them.

Ledarius wasn't that bothered by it, but he had wished a couple of times that she would stop staring at him and find something else to amuse herself with. Then just as he thought it, she stopped staring at him and began to dig in her nose and then very casually stuck her fingers in her mouth. Ledarius was disgusted but tried to focus on the case that was currently playing out in the courtroom.

"Now, Mister Andrews, what were you doing with two pounds of marijuana in the trunk of your grandmother's car?" the judge asked him. He leaned down towards the little microphone again, pulled up his pants, and responded in a voice that sounded very similar to the comedian Dave Chappelle. "I be smoking," he said as a few more people snickered underneath their breath. "You be smoking?" Judge Watkins responded with a shock in her voice that made everybody in the courtroom laugh.

"Why do you need to smoke so much marijuana Mister Andrews?" She asked in the sincerest voice she could muster. He pulled his pants up again and leaned down to put his mouth closer to the microphone again. "Sometimes I ask myself the same question," he replied. The whole courtroom erupted in laughter again, and at that point, even Judge Watkins tried her best to hold in a chuckle.

Judge Watkins looked down at her folder and said, "Mister Andrews, it says here that you told the arresting officer there were absolutely no illegal substances in the car whatsoever and then you—and I quote—'put that on your momma,' and when the officer pulled out the two pounds of marijuana, you said," she paused for dramatic effect and said, "It's medicinal." People had momentarily forgotten about their own cases and had now found themselves completely entertained by this one.

"Medicinal? Mister Andrews, is that right?" She looked down at him over her glasses. "Yup," he replied. "That's right. I got a birth defect." Everyone in the courtroom burst into laughter, and even Judge Watkins had to control herself. "Yeah, it comes and it goes," he added, using his Dave Chappelle voice again as everybody who was trying not to laugh earlier just had to.

"Well, Mister Andrews, that marijuana was a serious violation of your probation, so I'm afraid that I'm forced to send you back to juvie. Now, do you have any witty comebacks for that?" Judge Watkins said in a serious tone that made the courtroom go silent. "Nooo, wait," he cried out, "Nah, I can't go back right now man. I got stuff I got to do on Tuesday." A few people laughed, but now most of the people were whispering for him to shut up.

"Well, I'm sorry about your plans for Tuesday Mister Andrews, 'cause I think you're going to have to reschedule. Maybe you should have thought of that before you were caught with two pounds of marijuana in the trunk of your grandmother's car. Now you will have to serve out the rest of your probation in custody for the next eight months," she concluded and was ready to proceed to the next case.

"See, the system is designed to destroy us," Demarcus shouted as they walked him away. "Mister Andrews, the system, as you put it, does not have to be all that well designed to catch you in its web. Just look at yourself and the choices you're making. You're making it easy for 'the system'—she put it in quotes with the finger gesture— "to snatch you off the streets Mister Andrews. Next case!" she shouted.

After sitting through case after case and hearing story after story and sentence after sentence, they finally got around to Ledarius and called his name. "Ledarius Tate," Judge Watkins said after taking a sip from her coffee container. Ledarius stood up and made his way towards the aisle, and then through the swinging wooden double doors leading to the podium that stood in front of the judge's desk.

The judge smiled at Ledarius and began looking through the paperwork. Ledarius was sixteen and handsome for his age. He had what his teacher referred to as pleasant eyes. Although he was still young and growing, all the years of training had given him a muscular frame and well-defined features.

Judge Watkins was acquainted with the family for having previously presided over the cases when DeQuan had gotten himself into trouble. The younger of the two brothers had a colorful history and had been through these doors on several occasions. Judge Watkins knew that Ledarius was more of the good kid who had just gotten caught up in a bad situation.

"Have you been staying out of trouble Mister Tate?" she asked with a stern voice.

"Yes your honor," Ledarius replied.

"You know, Mister Tate, there are plenty of traps and pitfalls out here just waiting for young men just like yourself to constantly fall into." She spoke directly to him now and watched to make sure that she had his undivided attention. A man of Asian descent entered the back of the courtroom and sat down quietly in the back row.

"Yes, your honor," Ledarius replied again.

"And if you want to avoid them, you must be diligent, Mr. Tate, swift and resourceful. Do you understand me?" she said while looking directly at him again.

"Yes, your honor," Ledarius answered as she took another sip from her silver coffee mug.

Judge Watkins who has a son that once took classes with Master Yang read his charges out for the courtroom. "Now, I have been following this case very closely, and even though these are some serious charges Mister Tate, upon going over the details and taking into consideration the circumstances as well as other factors, I do believe that there is still hope for you. So, I am going to put you on six months of probation, and Mr. Yang, your former martial arts instructor, has asked if you could serve out your community service at the Rec Center, where you will be working for the duration of the summer. Am I making myself very clear to you Mister Tate?"

"Yes your honor," Ledarius responded.

"Good because the next time I see you in my courtroom, you better just be here to visit and thank me for how generous I'm being right now. So, you go on now and get out of here and have a productive summer, Mister Tate," she said, hitting her gavel. Then she gave Cynthia the subliminal mother-to-mother eye contact and nod.

Cynthia stood up and waited for Ledarius, and then they headed toward the back of the courtroom to leave. They met up with Master Yang, who had slipped in a few minutes earlier, in the hallway. Master Yang had been Ledarius's sensei since he was nine, and because of his reputation in the community as someone who helped countless kids over the years stay off the streets and knowing Judge Watkins personally for several years, he was able to use his influence to get Ledarius a much lighter sentence, for which his mother Cynthia was grateful.

"Well, thank you again Mr. Yang," Cynthia said giving him a hug.

"Yes, thanks Sensei," Ledarius echoed, giving him a fist bump.

"Anything I can do for you Ledarius, you know that. I will see you next week," he said as they all got into the elevator and rode to the first floor. Then, they walked through the lobby and outside. They said their goodbyes and headed their separate ways.

"Now, where the hell did I leave my car?" Cynthia stood with a confused expression on her face, scanning the parking lot with her eyes.

"It's over here Ma," Ledarius said, leading the way as she searched through her purse for her car keys. "C'mon, we about to stop by your Aunt Linda's before we go home."

Once they sat in the car, Cynthia turned and gave Ledarius a tight hug, and then she rubbed the top of his head and looked at him for a second. Afterward, she turned and started her car up and flipped through the radio stations until she found a song she liked before she could actually begin driving.

When she hit WGCI and found Jeremih's "Oui," she screamed and turned it up. "Oh yeah, Ah yeah, Ah yeah, Ah yeah!!" They pulled out of the parking spot abruptly and was on their way.

When they pulled up to Aunt Linda's house, Cynthia told Ledarius to wait in the car. A few seconds later, she fumbled through her purse for a second before she hopped out, slammed the door behind her, and then she walked around the car towards Linda's front gate. "Heyy girl!" she yelled as she waved to one of Aunt Linda's neighbors who was always outside sitting on her front porch minding everyone else's business. She disappeared inside the front door and Ledarius started to change stations when he heard a tap on the window.

"What's up Ledarius?" a fat kid who spoke as if his tongue was too big for his own mouth was at the window looking inside.

"What's up Snacks?" Ledarius said, rolling down the window.

"Yo, did you hear about dem niggas that got shot up on 83rd last night? Man, dudes was out there just trying to exist, and muthafuckas pulled up and just started busting. *Pop! Pop! Pop! Pop! Pop!*" Snacks said as he held his hand up in the air, pretending to pull the imaginary trigger of an invisible gun. "Niggas was running and ducking and screaming and cursing. A few niggas tried to shoot back, but they ain't hit shit tho, I don't think.

Where your brother at?" he asked, changing the subject completely without any warning whatsoever. "At school," Ledarius replied. "Nah uh, that boy ain't in school. I just left school. He wasn't there today. He wasn't there yesterday. He wasn't there on Wednesday." He started counting on his fingers. "He wasn't there on Tuesday. He was only there for about twenty minutes on Monday, and then he jumped in the car with Moochie and Kaos, and they was out," he added, looking at Ledarius for a response. "Not good," Ledarius said. "Not good is right," Snacks replied as if he had finally got what he had hoped for.

"Why you all dressed up? Is you practicing for Easter or something?" Snacks asked with a serious expression across his face, looking intently at Ledarius inside the car. "I had court this morning," Ledarius replied, pushing Snacks by his face back out of the car window.

"Oh shit. It musta' went ok if your black ass still sitting here, huh?" Snacks said, looking at Ledarius as if he was waiting for a response before he proceeded to say, "Shit, I got court next week for animal cruelty and indecent exposure," he said, scratching his head. "Muthafuckas tried to say they saw me running around the back alley behind old lady Loraine house with my Pee Pee out trying to piss on a kitten," he explained, looking confused as if he couldn't understand why somebody would say such a thing.

"Why would you even be trying to do that," Ledarius started to say when Snacks looked down the street and said, "Hold on, I gotta go," and ran off down the block towards his destiny. Ledarius looked out the passenger side window after him because he had never seen Snacks move that fast before.

"C'mon, let's go," Cynthia said as she jumped back into the car, turned on the ignition, and searched the radio again until she found her song and pulled off to Rihanna's "Needed Me." On the way home, they stopped by Pete's Produce on 87th Street and picked up a couple of things for Cynthia to cook for dinner. When they finally arrived at the house, Ledarius quickly helped his mom put up the groceries they had just bought, and immediately afterward he changed his clothes and went up to the roof of their apartment where he had a spot set up where he could go to meditate and practice.

Ledarius had recently begun to gain more mass and definition in his little muscles over the last few months and nowadays found himself flexing more and more in the mirror he had set up. He had his phone connected to a blu- tooth speaker and was playing a Chicago Classics playlist that currently was bumping Twista's hit song Adrenaline Rush featuring Yungbuck, not that guy from G-Unit, no disrespect, but I'm talking about the real Yungbuck from Psychodrama.

Ledarius practiced for a while until he was interrupted when he heard his mother yelling from the kitchen. "Momma, what's the matter?" Ledarius asked as he was coming through the window like a ninja.

"Your brother and his little lying ass ain't been to school all ghat damn week," Cynthia hollered and looked over at Ledarius. "Do you hear the words that are coming out of my mouth?" she said in her Chris Tucker voice. "At all…at all," she hollered again as she lit her cigarette and took a puff. "The little muthafucka ain't been to school AT ALL," she screamed out, hardly able to believe it. "And this little muthafucka been coming up in here every day like he coming from school, like he all tired and shit," Cynthia continued, and then she blew the smoke out from her cigarette, and just at that moment, they both heard the front door unlock. They both looked at each other and then back at the front door.

3.

DeQuan

"Oh, so it's some big conspiracy against you huh?" -
Cynthia

D eQuan walked into the house as if he had just gotten off of a
flight in Hawaii. "Hey y'all," he said with a big Kool-Aid
smile on his face, and then he looked at his mother's face and
then over at Ledarius, and then he looked back at his mother, and his
whole demeanor suddenly changed. He walked over and put his book
bag down on the chair and let out a huge sigh of relief. "Whew, I'm tired
from all that learning they had us doing today. Boy, math and science,
you know I really gotta hand it to 'em. They really stepped up the
curriculum this year," he said. He looked at his mother, then at Ledarius,
and he knew something was up.

"What's going on y'all?" Quan said in his calm voice, trying to
check the temperature in the room.

"I'll tell you what the hell is going on boy," Cynthia snapped. "Your ghat damn school just called here, and you know what they said?" Cynthia hit her cigarette and eye-bald Quan.

"I have the slightest idea momma," DeQuan said sarcastically but in a serious way.

"They said that yo little narrow ass ain't been to school all week." Quan looked at his mother with the most puzzled look on his face.

"*Whaat?*" he said as if he couldn't believe what he was hearing. "I'm trying to figure out why they would say something like that momma."

"Boy, don't try to stand there and act like this is all news to you," Cynthia snapped. It was the last week of school before summer vacation, so it wasn't really a big deal. "Momma can I get in the door good first, and then we can sit down and get to the bottom of this?" Quan responded.

"I wonder is it too late for me to get an abortion?" Cynthia spat and looked as if she was really considering the possibilities in her head.

"Momma I'm just as confused as you are. This gotta be some kinda mix-up. Let me go on down to the school and have a talk with these guys, and I'm sure we can get this whole thing squared away." DeQuan had been watching the movie "Goodfellas" a lot lately and had mysteriously adopted an Italian alter ego he came up with in his mind, and sometimes, he had a hard time knowing when to turn it off.

"That's it, no more Goodfellas, no more Scarface, and no more Godfather," Cynthia shouted. "Ledarius, go get all of them DVDs outta there, every one of 'em, 'cause you about to make me hurt you little boy." Ledarius left to do what his mother asked him.

"Momma, violence never solves anything," DeQuan explain in his innocent voice. "Violence solves a whole lotta shit boy," Cynthia fiercely shot back.

"Momma see, that's the problem with black folks; we're too reactionary," he said as he reached into his pocket, pulled out a stack of bills, folded some up, and stuck it in Cynthia's purse. "Momma these allegations that the school is making is bogus. It's all really just speculation. The nerve of these people momma, I'm offended, and you should be too, accusing yo baby..." He stood there shaking his head and looking puzzled, as if he was really thinking of how this could've happened.

"Boy, if you don't get yo ass out my face," Cynthia warned him.

"Momma, you don't even got all the facts! You just taking they side. They haven't even presented any proof." Quan tried it.

"Oh, so it's all just some big conspiracy against you, huh?" Cynthia said, taking a pull on her cigarette and pointing it at him.

"That's what I been saying, and my suspicions say that it must run pretty deep...we can't trust nobody Momma. I think they all in on it," he whispered as he looked around the room suspiciously.

Cynthia took a deep breath. "Boy, if you don't get the hell on somewhere, I swear I'm about to cook, and your little ass is the last thing I wanna see." Cynthia put an end to the conversation.

"I can make that happen momma, watch." Quan turned around, shook his head one more time, and then swiftly exited the kitchen. Ledarius looked at his mom and left right behind him.

After escaping his mother's wrath, Quan went into the bedroom he and Ledarius shared, went into the closet, pulled out a Nike AF1 shoebox, and sat down on the edge of the bed. He started pulling out large amounts of folded-up cash from different pockets and laid them all out. Then he reached into his sock and pulled out a bag about the size of a golf ball of crack cocaine and put it inside the shoebox. He pulled a gun from his waist, popped the shell out of the chamber, and put that underneath his mattress. Afterward, he made stacks of 1's, 5's, 10's, and 20's and started matching the rest of the bills to their respective stacks.

"Hey, did you know that Snacks...?" Ledarius started to say before Quan sharply cut him off.

"I don't wanna think about Snacks right now Ledarius," Quan said as he counted the money he had made and didn't want Ledarius to break his concentration. "Talk to me about something else," he told Ledarius, reassuring him that it was ok to talk, just not about that right now.

"They gave me probation and community service at court today. Master Yang set it up so I could work with him at the Rec, where he has the temporary Dojo setup." Ledarius told his brother, who had seemed to totally block him out as he was counting the money on his bed, moving his lips quietly with each bill he pulled from the stack.

"Cool," Quan responded a few seconds later after he was done counting, letting his brother know he was listening all along. "You can get that probation street cred going for you, so people won't think you such a lame when you get up there and shit," Quan explained, trying in his own way to be reassuring.

Quan and Ledarius had different fathers. Quan's father was a drug dealer from 79th and Marshfield back in the day, along with his cousin, who everybody called Big Heat. His father was the brains, and Heat was the muscle. Quan's father had built up a dope spot that was making over five thousand a day. One night, after a night of partying, some niggas kicked the door off the hinges and ran in with shotguns and pistols and tried to rob the spot. Quan's father grabbed his gun and shot two of the robbers, but he was hit himself a couple of times and started bleeding pretty badly until a girlfriend who was there was able to get him out of the house and to the hospital.

When Big Heat found out, he rushed to the hospital in a rage, and when he saw his cousin, all shot up and clinging to life, he lost it. Thinking his cousin wasn't going to make it, he rushed out for revenge on everybody he thought had something to do with it. When he tracked down the ones he thought was responsible, he went crazy and killed everyone onsite.

When the police arrived, Big Heat was still at the scene and got into a bloody shootout with Chicago Police. He was shot twenty eight times and pronounced dead at the scene. Quan's father, a short time later, recovered from his injuries to find his cousin had been killed while avenging him. He went back to work and tried to get back to where he was before the robbery. But a year later, he was caught with five kilos of cocaine and sentenced to prison. While he was incarcerated, the police pinned a murder on him, stemming from the retaliation for his cousin, and gave him life without the possibility of parole.

Quan was a troubled child pretty much as soon as he learned to walk. He often had mood swings and violent fits of rage. When he was around five, he began torturing small animals, and once he started school, he began to terrorize classmates, teachers and faculty.

When he was seven, he witnessed a murder in the alley behind his grandmother's house and was catatonic for three whole days while Cynthia and Ledarius waited for him to snap out of it. When he came to, he had abandoned all his previously troubled behavior—for a while anyway.

When Quan was eight, he started hanging out on the block, and that's when him and his best friend Stimey starting getting into shit, and began recruiting other little bad ass kids to do shit with them. Because he knew how to fight and how to carry himself, he eventually gained the respect of the older dudes in the neighborhood; plus it didn't hurt that most of them knew who his father was.

Then, two summers ago, a war broke out on the Southside between rival gangs, and it was rumored that he and a group of his friends that some people called "The Rug Rat Mafia," because of how young they all were, had taken part in a string of unsolved homicides, but that was only a rumor.

One of the young soldiers who worked for Quan's father's organization was a guy named Moochie, and after they were out of the way, Moochie grew in power and started calling himself The General. Then, he started his own organization, and eventually, he recruited Quan to work for him. Quan, because of his family ties, his heart, and his street smarts, eventually became one of Moochie's right hands, and was sometimes even seen riding around with him in Moochie's Georgetown blue, 1983 Chevy Caprice Classic, which was the reason he hadn't been to school all week.

"What?" Quan asked, looking at Ledarius. "You looking like you judging me, don't judge me Darri, only God can judge me, ya dig, and the last time I checked, you was not him. yo black ass didn't create the moon and sea." he commented and then he chuckled to himself. Sometimes Quan liked to hear himself talk. Ledarius smirked and dismissed his brother's trash talk and his perfectly integrated Tupac reference.

"What Darri? Am I supposed to let the Chicago public school system teach me how to govern my intellectual and spiritual evolution? Is that what you want me to do bruh? seriously? Is that what you want for me? To be a slave to the man, jack?" Quan said, speaking in the voice of one of his many characters in amusement to only himself.

Ledarius liked seeing his brother playing and joking around because it meant that, in that moment, he was happy, which was a good thing. DeQuan kept talking, but Ledarius was more concerned about the community service he had to go to on Monday. He hadn't been to Master Yang's class since he had gotten into trouble, but he was anxious to get back in, even if he wasn't exactly a student.

4.

The Rec

"Now what's a handsome young man like yourself doing getting into all that trouble?" -Miss Freeman

On Monday, Ledarius went to the Rec Center, where Master Yang had a temporary Dojo set up after the original Dojo caught on fire a few months ago due to faulty wiring. He walked in and looked around for whom he was supposed to check in with. "Hey, what can I do for you, young brother?" a clean-cut and athletically built dude in his mid-twenties asked Ledarius from behind the front desk.

Marcus had grown up in the neighborhood, and after getting into trouble and going to jail, he got out and turned his life around. He was now a single father raising his five-year-old daughter by himself and staying as far away from trouble as possible. He and Miss Freeman, an older woman in her late fifties who had been at that recreation center for over twenty years, ran the front desk.

"I'm supposed to work here for the summer. My name is Ledarius Tate," Ledarius introduced himself.

"Oh, that's right, you're the one that's doing your community service here?" Miss Freeman said, looking at him over her tiny square-framed bifocals.

"Yes ma'am," Ledarius humbly replied.

"Now, what's a handsome young man like yourself doing getting into all that trouble?" Miss Freeman said, looking closely at Ledarius.

"Yeah, 'cause a handsome young man like yourself might wanna try to avoid prison, bruh," Marcus said to his own amusement, and Miss Freeman quickly shushed him.

Ledarius gave Marcus a quick look and asked if they knew where he could find Master Yang.

Just then, a young, bright-skinned kid of about 11-years-old, wearing a Rajon Rondo LA Lakers Jersey walked up and said, "What up, Marcus?… Hey, Miss Freeman." He held his hand out to fist-bump Marcus, and then he looked Ledarius up and down. "What's up, man? You new around here?" he asked, looking at Ledarius like he was sizing him up.

"Yes, I am looking for Master Yang," Ledarius responded.

"Ooh, you mean the Karate Room? Yeah, it's that way." The kid pointed his finger toward the hallway and then started talking to Marcus, completely ignoring Ledarius.

"Ahhh, Dajon, can you be a sport and take Ledarius here and show him where the gym is?" Miss Freeman interrupted.

"What?" Dajon responded. "I hope this new addition to my job description comes with a hefty pay bump," he replied, getting smart with Miss Freeman.

"Boy, I'm going to give you a hefty pay bump alright, if you don't take this boy over there to Mr. Yang," she shot back.

"Okay, okay, now that this is becoming a hostile environment. Come on, I got you. I'm headed that way anyway, because that's where I hear the money calling from." He put his hand to his ear as if he were listening for something, and then he flashed a bright smile and signaled for Ledarius to follow him. "Now, usually, I would charge for my time, but I'm feeling generous today, so you're in luck, my man," he told Ledarius and sized him up again one more time.

Dajon sold candy at the Rec Center. It was rumored that he had disabled all the vending machines in the building to eliminate the competition, but he said that was just speculation. He was the son of a hustler and had picked up the knack for making a quick buck early. His father was killed along with his uncle a few years ago in front of their house while Dajon sat in a car across the street and watched the whole thing as it happened.

"My name is Dajon. If you ever need a sugar rush, come holla atcha' boy." He started rapping. "Last time I checked, I was the man on these streets. I leave Kit Kats and Twinkies residue on these beats." He made a couple of mean faces while moving his hands around. "See, I was in Atlanta once with my man Young Jeezy, you know? And I let him hear my jingle or whatever, you know? So, dig, he took it and flipped it and put his own little spin on it or whatever and put it out on a record. He ain't cut me no check, no publishing, not even a shout-out. You see how negros do you?" Dajon added with the utmost seriousness.

"First of all, I'm pretty sure you don't know Young Jeezy, and also, I know for a fact that you wasn't even born yet when that record even came out," Marcus replied to Dajon, debunking his story, which seemed to slightly annoy him. "Man, everything ain't always gotta make sense to you, Marcus." He made a face and laughed, and then everybody else laughed, including Marcus.

"Go on now and take this boy to his class Dajon before I give you that pay bump across your forehead" Miss Freeman ordered. "Okay Okay, I know when to remove myself from a hostile environment" Dajon responded, then he told Ledarius to follow him and they turned to leave. They walked through a couple of hallways until they happened to walk past an open door to where the girls' dance club was, they girls were warming up for class as the sound of music and chattering spilled out of the room.

Ledarius looked through the cracked door at the dozen or so girls listening to music and talking amongst themselves, and occasionally busting out an impromptu dance move or two. There was a short, light-skinned girl with cornrows on the side of the stage controlling the music and three or four other girls on the stage working on a dance routine.

The girl on the stage that caught his attention was a vision of pure beauty. Ledarius thought he was looking at an actual angel on earth. She had a belly button ring that focused even more attention on her flat washboard abs and a smooth caramel complexion. She had hazel eyes and long golden braids that hung down, covering her perfect neck and shoulders. She was obviously the star of the group, and her energy showed it. Then she looked over and noticed him standing there.

Ledarius felt a pinhole in his heart that expanded to the size of a dinner plate instantly. It was as if a volcano had erupted in his chest and blew hot lava out all over the inside of his body. He had seen beautiful girls before, but they were not like her. She looked like she came from another planet, where everybody was beautiful and she was the stand out.

What he was feeling now, at this very moment, was what every boy feels at some point in his life when he first lays eyes on the girl of his dreams. Suddenly, Dajon grabbed him by the arm and pulled him out of there and down the hall towards Master Yang's makeshift Dojo. He opened the door to the gym, walked inside, and looked around. "I ain't never did Karate before, but my uncle used to box in the amateurs. He even went to the golden gloves and everything," Dajon explained. "He showed me a thing or two, so don't get it twisted now. Your boy is nice with the hands, okay?" Dajon continued with young confidence.

"Ledarius, glad to have you with us," Master Yang said as he saw Ledarius and Dajon approaching from across the gymnasium.

"Greetings, Master Yang," Ledarius said.

"Hey, Master Yang," Dajon echoed.

"Dajon, are you here to join our class?" Master Yang asked.

"Nah, I'm good. I'm just here directing traffic for slave wages," Dajon said as he threw up the deuces. "See you later, Ledarius Sun," he said jokingly with the Karate Kid reference. Then, he turned around and left back to where he had heard the money calling from earlier.

Students began coming into the gym, talking to one another and horse-playing around. Everybody lined up once they were done, and Master Yang was about to introduce Ledarius to the class. Then, four or five boys walked in late after everyone was already in place. "Class, this is Ledarius. He was one of my finest pupils and a fierce warrior. I had the pleasure of training him for many years. He will be joining us and assisting in our lessons."

One of the boys who entered class late said something under his breath, and a couple of his friends laughed, which caught Master Yang's attention. "Maine, is there anything that you would like to share with the rest of the class before we get started?" They all straightened up. "No, Sensei," the student quickly replied.

As the boys took their places, one of them recognized Ledarius with a head nod. "Who is that?" one of the boys asked. "That's Ledarius. He used to go to the old Dojo, but then he just stopped coming. Some kinda trouble, I think."

They began class that day with Master Yang pulling Ledarius out in front of the class to demonstrate certain techniques. "Ole' teacher's pet-looking ass boy," one of the boys said while deciding that he wasn't going to like Ledarius.

Ledarius got more and more comfortable as the class went on. Hearing Master Yang's voice again gave him a sense of normalcy. The workouts jogged his memory and helped him get back into the routine. He thought about how lucky he was to be here and not at a standard community service site. Then, the picture of the angelic girl from the dance class earlier filled his mind, and his heart followed right along. He couldn't wait until class was over so he could see her again. Ledarius was feeling things he wasn't exactly used to feeling, and he knew that once he saw her again, those feelings were going to grow.

When class was finally over, the kid who recognized Ledarius earlier came over. "What's up, "Jet Ledarius?" he said, emphasizing each syllable as he shook his hand and pulled him in for a bro hug.

"Glad to see you back." He continued, Ledarius smiled and bowed, and then they shook hands. "Jacob my friend, it is good to see you as well, but I'm mostly here to assist Master."

They spoke briefly until Jacob had to go. "I'll catch up with you tho. Tell your brother I said what's up," he said as he walked off to catch up with the rest of his friends who were leaving. Ledarius stayed behind to sweep up and put away the equipment. He thought about the time he spent away from Master Yang and all that he learned during that time from another Master, who was a female friend of Master Yang's that he had known for some time. Master Yang had suggested that Ledarius help her do some work in her garden for a small weekly pay.

When he finally finished up and left, he walked down the hallway and felt excitement in his chest, which could only be described as pure bliss. He approached the door of the dance class, just dying to look inside, but everyone had already left. He felt his whole ship sink. She was gone. He sadly turned around and left. On his way out, he walked past the front desk.

Miss Freeman was entrenched in a very serious game of Candy Crush on her phone with Marcus standing behind her, singing and dancing to LL Cool J's "Pink Cookies in A Plastic Bag Getting Crushed by Buildings." Miss Freeman crushed away on her phone and eventually joined in with some dance moves of her own.

Marcus kept singing and dancing until Ledarius walked up. "What can I do for you, young man?" he asked Ledarius, completely out of character from what he had just been doing literally seconds before.

"Am I interrupting something?" Ledarius asked reluctantly.

"Yes," Miss Freeman replied. "You didn't give him time to do his LL Cool J lips," she said, disgruntled, as Marcus stood next to her, posing and licking his lips like he was LL Cool J back in the days.

"Look, child," Miss Freeman said taking a break from her game. "Go out there with everybody else and make some new friends," she advised Ledarius. "Yeah, but make sure they're not the type of friends that's gonna get you into trouble 'cause remember, you don't wanna go to jail," Marcus added, totally amused by his own dark, twisted humor.

When Ledarius stepped out into the bright sunlight, he spotted her. He walked towards the benches and sat down across from where she and her friends were hanging out. He tried to occupy himself by looking down at his shoes, but he couldn't keep himself from staring at her. Then Dajon walked up and sat on the bench next to him, threw his book bag down, and noticed what Ledarius was looking at.

"Oh, that's Brooklyn. She AK's girl," he said. "You might wanna leave her alone 'cause them guys ain't for play play. They got their hands in everything from underground fight clubs to cracking cars. I even heard they be doing hits on people for the mob, so unless you trying to get fucked up…" he was saying, but Ledarius had begun to tune him out and

40

picture the two of them rushing into each other's arms in slow motion, just like in the movies.

Brooklyn was with her usual crew of "It" girls, which consisted of the twins Tenishia and Camisha, who were a force to be reckoned with on the dance floor. There was a Black and Puerto Rican girl Vanessa, whose nickname was "Vanessa the finesser" because she could finesse a nigga out of anything. It was once said that she finessed a dude out of his White Sox jersey. She just walked up to him and asked him for it, and he took it off and gave it to her, and then she put it on over her shirt and walked around with it on for absolutely no reason. Then there was Alikah, the African princess, who was a dark-skinned bombshell with model-like good looks, and then there was her BFF Cali. Brooklyn and Cali had been best friends since the second grade.

Brooklyn was the type of girl that you either loved or were jealous of. But even then, she was so nice and sweet to everyone that you would just say fuck it and be nice to her even if you really didn't like her all that much. Brooklyn and her girls were inseparable, and if you had a problem with one of them, then you had a problem with all of them They were the core of the dance club and the stars of Recreation center and everybody knew it.

5.

Brooklyn

"I am no longer looked at with lechery or love" -Brooklyn

Brooklyn was raised taking piano lessons and ballet. Not because her family was wealthy but because her mother was determined to give her daughter every tool she thought she could need to succeed in life. She was raised reading books and learning what it took to be a successful and strong Black woman in today's society. She learned the history of strong black women like Nina Simone and Angela Davis to Michelle Obama and Cathy Hughes.

Once, when Brooklyn was in the second grade, she had to recite a poem of her choice to the entire classroom. Brooklyn was nervous, but she also didn't want to chicken out, so she chose the poem "A Sunset of the City" by Gwendolyn Brooks. She practiced and practiced each day until the day finally came for her to get up in front of the entire class and overcome her fear.

"Already, I am no longer looked at with lechery or love," she began. As she continued, two girls began to ignore her and started talking and laughing to themselves. A short, light-skinned girl in the back of the room named Cassandra stood up and told everybody to shut up and be quiet, and she looked at Brooklyn and said, "Spit that." She sat back down, not knowing that at that very moment, she had made a friend for life, as Brooklyn finished her poem with confidence.

In the third grade, they were inseparable. They sat next to each other in class and ate lunch together every day. They hung out at each other's house on the weekends. That was the year Cassandra had a crush on Brandon Ross, but Brandon liked Brooklyn, and Cassandra was so scared that they were going to date, which would have left her completely devastated. But when Brooklyn found out, she told Brandon that if he didn't like her friend, he could never be her friend either, or anything with her for that matter, and that was that.

In the fourth grade, they won a 90's-themed costume party, and they were dressed as the pop singer Aaliyah and Left Eye from the group TLC. With Brooklyn being a natural dancer and Cassandra finding her voice, the two sealed the deal with an impromptu performance of waterfalls, with Brooklyn switching roles to play T Boz and Chilli and Cassandra delivering in her role as Left Eye.

In the fifth grade, Cassandra's father and uncle were murdered in front of their house while Cassandra was upstairs in her bedroom. Her younger cousin was outside in the car across the street, waiting for his father and uncle to finally take him along with them after constantly begging them for weeks.

After that tragedy struck her family, Cassandra's mother asked Brooklyn's mother, Nicole, if Cassandra could stay with them and go to school with Brooklyn while they were dealing with everything, and Nicole agreed. So, Cassandra moved in for the rest of the school year and most of the summer until she just picked up one day and said she was ready to go home.

In the sixth grade, Cassandra's older brother, a local DJ at the time, who went by the name of DJ J Sinister, convinced her to do a freestyle over Snoop Dogg's "Ain't Nuthin' but a G Thang" beat, and the rest was history. Her older brother had made such a big deal over the verse she kicked that Cassandra knew she wanted to rap from that day on. During Cassandra's freestyle, she referred to herself as "Cali Cassanova," and the name stuck.

That same year, Brooklyn was beginning to glow up and started attracting a lot of attention from the boys and the females who were jealous of it. Donisha Coley got a bunch of her friends to follow Brooklyn and Cali into the girls' bathroom right before lunch. Donisha had been planning to fight Brooklyn all week and had reached her boiling point when she thought Brooklyn was flirting with a boy she liked. When Donisha approached her, she shouted, "Oh bitch, no, you're not." She and four of her friends followed Brooklyn and Cali into the girls' bathroom and blocked the exit so no one could go in or out.

Brooklyn and Cali were in the back of the bathroom with five girls between them and the door. They were left with no choice, so they had to fight. When Brooklyn started beating up Donisha, the other girls tried to help her, and Cali jumped in and started stabbing the girls with the pencil she used to write her rhymes with. Brooklyn pulled out a bottle of lavender body spray and started spraying bitches in the face at first, and eventually, she started beating them with the bottle until it broke.

The fight that took place in the bathroom that day was legendary. It was two against five, and the fact that they were still on their feet at the end of it all and the girls who jumped them ended up more fucked up than them, made them instantly more popular.

Eight grade year was a breeze after the big bathroom brawl the year before. People just sort of became more friendly. Cali had won the school talent show that year, and Brooklyn started her first dance crew to back her up. They were big shots now and loving every minute of it while they got ready to graduate and take on the most brutal battle of all—high school.

A few weeks after graduation, Cali's brother was killed in a car crash caused by a police officer who was speeding with his lights on to get through a traffic light and ran into the car he was riding in. He suffered multiple injuries and was taken to Cook County, where he was later pronounced dead. The officer was not in pursuit of anyone and was never charged with any wrongdoing.

The local Hip Hop community was devastated because everybody knew that J Sinister was going to blow up one day. Pastor AD, who was once a troubled teen himself on the streets before he turned his life around, had suggested to Cali's mother that he thought it would be a good idea for Cali and her younger cousin to go and join the local Rec Center. There, his long-time friend and member of the church, Miss Freeman, ran a program geared towards helping children that had been through traumatic circumstances in life, giving them a safe place to get help and resources and, most of all, according to Miss Freeman, love.

Freshman year at Whitney Young had reduced them back to small fish in a large pond and reset the game back to zero. When Cali finally agreed to go and give the Rec Center a try, Brooklyn went along with her friend for support, and once Brooklyn found out that the dance teacher Kaleena Ray, who was a former Chicago Bulls cheerleader, was teaching classes there, she couldn't resist and signed them both up for the dance class, and the rest was history.

Now, back in the present, they were both here trying to figure out what old-school song to dance to for this week's dance challenge, where the girls had to choose a popular song from the 80's and develop a modern dance routine. The winner got the spotlight of the big 4th of July Showcase, which was a huge deal that year because it would be streaming live for the first time.

"Brooklyn, I think you have an admirer, bitch!" Vanessa said with a smirk on her face looking in the direction of the new boy. When Brooklyn looked over, she pointed toward Dajon and Ledarius. Brooklyn glanced over towards Ledarius for a quick second and continued her freestyle dance routine, putting a little extra sauce on it now that she knew she had somebody watching.

"I saw him earlier when he first came in. Girl, he is a whole meal," Teneshia said, looking at Ledarius and biting on her bottom lip.

"Oh, he can definitely get it," Camisha chimed in.

"Girl, I hope he falls off the back of that bench right now and hits his head real hard on a rock or something, so I can run over there and give him mouth-to-mouth resuscitation for like thirty-five or forty-five minutes." They all laughed, and Brooklyn turned toward her friend.

"Misha, I'm going to need you to focus on not being such a hoe, okay girl?" Brooklyn said sarcastically.

"High Hoe, High Hoe, off the porch we go." Misha began to sing the song from Snow White and the Seven Dwarfs, and then they all began to join in and harmonize. Even Cali joined in when it came to the part where they all whistled. Brooklyn took another glance over towards Ledarius and Dajon, who, for some reason, was in the middle of some sort of break-dancing routine.

Then, the group of boys who had come late to class earlier had walked out and strolled right over to where Brooklyn and her girls were. The one in charge was named Andre Kennedy, or AK for short. He always had the same group of boys with him, Psyke, Maine, and Fang. Fang was Korean and Black and was cocky, like a young version of Bolo Yeung from the movie "Enter the Dragon" who went at it with Bruce Lee. He was also said to have actually trained with Tony Jaa who played in Ong Bak, and then there was his right-hand man Tick, which was short for Lunatic. Tick was the heart-throb of the bunch, and all the girls wanted to give him some. He was brown skinned, tall, and built with hard eyes that made girls go crazy.

"Yo', what you bust downs got going on over here?" Tick asked Cali as he sat down between the twins and put his arm around both of them.

"Who you calling bust downs tho? You over here looking like a tough R&B singer. Boy, get the fuck outta here." She squared up with him like she was about to punch him.

"We checking out Brooklyn's finna be new boo," Camisha replied.

"Whaaat?" Tick followed Camisha's eyes over to Ledarius.

AK played it off, but he looked to see who they were talking about. "What you mean, that lame ass nigga over there? You fuck with lame niggas now? Oh, okay." Tick Laughed. He knew AK wasn't going to say anything, so he said everything for him. "That nigga soft as wet toilet paper. You need a real boss." Cali lit the blunt she had just finished rolling.

"Well, I guess that excludes you then, don't it?" She smiled at Tick and blew smoke at him.

AK gave the signal to Tick, and he and the rest of the clique got up to leave. AK looked at Brooklyn as he walked by, and her eyes followed his as if to say, "What?" but she already knew. He had liked her since he first moved into the area, and at one point, they were almost about to be a couple, but Brooklyn, being Brooklyn, pulled back at the last minute and had been elusive ever since.

AK and the boys weren't the ones to play with. They were dangerous, and what made them so dangerous was that they didn't move like other niggas. They read books, like The Art of War and studied martial arts. They were lethal with their fist but also had pistols and assault rifles. Can you imagine a nigga beating you up with a pair of nun chucks like Bruce Lee, and then whipping out a pistol and shooting you?

AK had a thing for Brooklyn, and everybody knew it. As long as Brooklyn wasn't messing with anybody, it was all cool but let somebody start trying to really get at her, it was probably going to be some static because everybody knew that was AK's girl.

They walked to AK's truck, which was a customized black and red chromed-out Escalade they nicknamed the Mother Ship. They jumped inside, and then they rolled by like they were either about to do a drive-by shooting or pull up and hop out and shoot a rap video. They got to the street and paused for dramatic effect. Then, they turned and sped off down the street bumping "This ain't what u want" by Lil Durk.

6.

Dajon

"I'm 11, and the way I look at it, life is all about
Mathematics" - Dajon

T he next day Ledarius helped Master Yang at the end of class.
"Ledarius, how was your time working with Master Wong?"
Master Yang asked as he helped put up the equipment.

"It went pretty good, I guess. I learned a lot from her over the year
that I was not with you, Master." He pulled the mats back to the wall and
stacked them one on top of the other. "I will be glad to see her when she
returns back from China." He pulled another mat from the middle of the
floor over to the wall and threw it on top of the pile. Once they were
finished, Master Yang went to his office and began to read over the
paperwork for the insurance claim for the Dojo.

Ledarius went out to the front to get some air and spotted Dajon
out there selling candy as usual. "Girl, you know you want these honey
buns?" he shouted. "What's up, Ledarius? Walk with me to the gas

station," Dajon insisted as he was already hopping off the bench and making his way.

As they walked down the street, they were approached by a crackhead selling a fake gold chain for the low. "Move around, man!" Dajon yelled at the ghetto crack jeweler. Dajon went inside the corner store to get a refill of the candy he needed. After he had collected everything off the list he had in his head—because he never wrote anything down—he put it all in his book bag and walked over to the counter.

The young Arab dude behind the counter shook Dajon's hand, and Dajon handed him a paper bag with who knows what inside. He asked Dajon how the tests went, and Dajon told him that he had aced them. He walked over to where Ledarius was waiting and said that they could leave.

"What test?" Ledarius asked when they got outside. "The guy in there asked you about some test," Ledarius asked Dajon as they walked back towards the Rec.

"Some math test at Kennedy King College for some early college courses or whatever," Dajon said as if it were nothing.

"Wow, you're taking college courses? You must be pretty smart then. How old are you?" They crossed the street towards the corner where the Rec was.

"I'm eleven, and the way I see it, Ledarius, life is all about mathematics." They walked past the Rec, and it seemed as if everyone had cleared out. "See, dudes is out here in the streets on their addition, you know, trying to get money to add to their pockets, but the system got them divided; that's division. But if the whole number moved as one, then their wealth and resources would multiply, see? Multiplication. But dudes don't see it like that, so we out here losing. You feel me? Dudes getting killed and going to jail and taking that loss—that, my friend, is subtraction," Dajon explained. "See, it's all mathematics."

"That's why Rajon Rondo is my favorite player, 'cause he was a math whiz in college before he went to the NBA, and that's why he can run the court the way he do. He stay calculating, you feel me?" He took his index finger and tapped the side of his head with it to drive home his point.

Ledarius was shocked that a little kid would say something like that. "You are a wise little Buddha," Ledarius said.

"Buddha? Whatchu' trying to buy some weed? Man, you shoulda told me when we was back there," Dajon replied.

"No. 'Buddha,' it means that you are very wise." They made it to the bus stop and sat down.

"Well, I don't know about Buddha, but I do know about Luda, and he is pretty wise too. He says, '*Move, bitch, get out the way, get out the way, bitch, get out the way.*" He rapped in his best Ludacris voice and made Ledarius chuckle. "Ayye, you know you want this Snickers," he yelled at some girls who were walking past. "Yo', I heard that boy AK killed his dad's best friend when he was 12. Now I don't know if it's true or not. I'm just telling you what I heard."

"Yo', Dajon, let me get a Kit Kat," a young kid around 9-years-old with big green eyes and curly brown hair said, walking up. His name was Bug, and he had on an Avatar the Last Airbender t-shirt and was fiddling

52

around in his pockets, searching for his change. "Yo', I only got $1.25 Lemme owe you a quarter," he tried to bargain.

"I don't give credit because credit collections can get messy, and the percentages ain't always worth the risk," Dajon said, giving his professional assessment.

"But I'll tell you what I'mma do, okay? I'm gonna give you this sweet, delicious Kit Kat, but you gon have to work the balance off. So, I'mma need you to make some sales, bring in some business, and learn the game in case I decide to retire someday," Dajon told him, and he handed him the Kit Kat. When Bug reached for it, Dajon pulled it back really quick. "Now, don't forget our deal because I don't wanna have to send my ninja right here to come for you to get that bread back, you feel me?" he added and then Dajon handed him the Kit Kat. "Now, you make sure you eat that real slow," Dajon said. A few minutes later, Dajon saw a 2016 Chevy Malibu pull up in the parking lot and park. He checked for his phone and told Ledarius to be careful out there and keep his head on a swivel. He gave him a fist bump and darted off in the direction of his ride.

Ledarius watched him get into the car, and then he got up and headed to the bus stop. On the way home, Ledarius seemed to drift off into his own thoughts. He thought about Brooklyn and how pretty her skin was and how soft her hair looked. His thoughts were abruptly interrupted by a half dozen police cars speeding by the bus heading in the opposite direction. There had been tension in the streets after police shot and killed an unarmed teen a few weeks earlier, and that wasn't the first time. Ledarius just wanted to get home. He wondered what his little brother was doing.

7.

The Royal Cabinet

"Don't be fucking with my squad, that's in the Bible" -
DeQuan

Quan was on the front porch of his and Ledarius's grandmother's house, which was right around the corner from their apartment. He was getting his hair re-twisted by a girl named Gigi, who grew up down the street and always had a crush on him. Quan and Gigi had known each other since the sandbox, and even though she was cute, he still had never really thought of her that way. Quan always kept his royal cabinet around, as he would call them sometimes, according to one of his many alter egos whenever he got high.

"We don't got no team no more because the suits in the front office over there making decisions while they high off the cocoa. How the hell you gon' go and trade off Rose and Noah?"

"What the fuck kinda sense do that make?" Lil Stimey said as he rolled up a blunt. Stimey and Quan have been best friends since before they could walk, literally. Cynthia and Stimey's mother, Jackie were friends who were both pregnant at the same time. Once their sons were born, they would have them both side by side in their strollers when they were at the mall or side by side strapped into their car seats when they shopped for groceries, and they have been riding together ever since.

"I know, right, and just when we finally had a fucking squad again." Quan added. "We never should've got rid of Nate Robinson. We should've kept him just to back Rose up, then maybe that nigga wouldn't break like a ghatdamn Christmas toy," Quan joked, and everybody laughed.

"They been making suspect decisions like that ever since the Jordan and Pippen days." Uncle June, who was older, but would always stop by the porch on his way to either here or there to ask for change to buy a beer or a hit of the blunt, adding in his two cents. "After we win a championship, they start trading people in the off-season. I mean we still won, but that was risky moves they were making."

"Right," Quan chimed in. "Fucking with the damn squad. That's why Golden State straight 'cause they don't trade off players all willy-nilly and shit. They add pieces, ghatdammit!" he shouted, and everybody started laughing 'cause they knew Quan was headed for his soap box.

"See them suits in the front office. They putting the dollar first. They don't respect what actually generates those dollars, which is the players. How you gon win if your soldiers don't fuck wit' you?" Everybody laughed. "They want all the golden eggs that the goose lay, but wanna say 'Fuck the goose.' I don't get the logic," Quan said, standing up after sitting down for so long, getting his hair re-twisted.

"See, they keep throwing off the chemistry 'cause they don't know the science. They think they know the science, but they don't know shit, 'cause they blinded by their own greed, my nigga." He hit the blunt and sang, "Greeeed" out loud like a young ghetto opera singer, and everybody laughed.

"Don't be fucking with my squad, that's in the Bible," Quan said with the utmost confidence.

"Boy, stop, that is not in no Bible." Gigi said.

"Yes, it is, it's in Corinthians," Quan snapped back to everybody's amusement.

"That is not in no damn Corinthians," Gigi said with a slight chuckle.

"When was the last time you read Corinthians?" Quan said and waited for a second. "Exactly, 'cause you don't know what the fuck is in Corinthians," Quan said as he dusted off his shirt. "You don't know what's in Corinthians," he pointed at Gigi, "and you don't know what's in Corinthians," he pointed at Uncle June, "and you don't know what's in Corinthians he pointed at Gigi's friend," he pointed again like Oprah Winfrey giving out cars, "and you definitely don't know what's in no muthafuckin' Corinthians he pointed at Stimey. Should anything be in there, wouldn't none of you muthafuckas know it. Ghatdamn infidels." He sat back down and hit the blunt, and everybody erupted in laughter.

DeQuan took out his phone to see if he had any missed calls, but he hadn't. He didn't think much of it, but he had not heard from Kaos in a minute after just recently plugging him in with Moochie. Quan decided that if he didn't hear from him soon, he would get a ride and go check on him.

8.

Nikki

"Lord, don't let my baby be a thot" - Nikki

When Brooklyn made it home later that day, she was greeted by her mother, Nicole, who was eating sushi and finishing up some work on her laptop. "Hey, Sugar B, how was your day today?" she asked with excitement in her voice as Brooklyn pulled out a chair and sat down at the dining room table across from her mother.

"We rehearsed some dances we had seen in some YouTube videos we watched, but we still haven't come up with a song for our performance yet," she replied as she looked over and grabbed a piece of sushi from her mother's plate and bit into it.

"Don't even worry about that. It will come to you, and when it does, you'll know it," Nicole responded as she made a confused face at her laptop screen. "How is your writing coming along?" Nicole asked while she examined her computer screen, took a bite of her sushi, and drank from her wine glass. "Okay, I guess," Brooklyn replied.

"Have you read Winter yet?" Nicole asked, closing her laptop down. "Nah, I haven't gotten around to it yet," she replied, embarrassed because she had told her mother for weeks now that she would get to it.

"Well, if you're going to be a writer, you might wanna read one of the best literary masterpieces by one of my favorite writers of all time, Sister Souljah."

"The Coldest Winter Ever" is one of my favorite books. Once you pick it up, you won't ever want to put it down. See, Winter was young and pretty like you are, but she was raised by a drug-dealing dad and a ghetto diva of a mother, and when it all fell apart, she had to do what she had to do the best way she knew how to survive." Nicole explained and looked over at Brooklyn to see if she was getting what she was telling her before she continued.

"Sister Souljah used to be a rapper and an activist. She was part of Public Enemy back in the day. You know who Public Enemy is, right?" she asked with a renewed facial expression. "Fight the power…Fight the power…Fight the power…we got to fight the powers that be," she said in a low voice, imitating the rapper Chuck D while dancing in a way that made Brooklyn watch until she suddenly wanted to cringe.

"Ok, I'll get around to it," Brooklyn said. "Okay, well, tell me when you do so I can re-read my copy, and we can read that bad boy together," she said as she ate another piece of her sushi and quickly typed some stuff out on her laptop.

"Now, I was listening to the radio on my way in to work this morning and I heard the Migos. You know who I'm talking about? The Migos? Those little rapper boys from Atlanta that try to sound like Bone," she said and took another sip from her wine glass. "And one of 'em said, your girl she a thot-thot-thot, you know what I'm talking about?" She looked Brooklyn in the face. Brooklyn could hardly contain her laughter. "Yes, they did, thot-thot-thot," she said as she did a little dance as if she were dancing to an imaginary beat. "Now, baby girl, I know you are not out here behaving in any way where someone can call you a thot-thot-thot, right?" she asked with her face becoming more serious, but in a playful way at the same time, and then repeating, "thot- thot-thot" as she again and bounced to an imaginary beat.

"Nooo," Brooklyn exclaimed, slightly embarrassed by her mother's question. "Beause Iet me tell you something right now. Don't ever, ever, ever, ever do nothing where somebody can say something about what you did, okay? You got to keep your shit on the down low. Your reputation is everything if you plan to rise up in life, okay? 'Thot-thot-thot.' Girl, when I found out what the word really meant, I said, Oh Lord, don't let my baby be a thot," she said in a loud tone resembling that of a church pastor while shaking her arms. Then she looked at her computer screen and turned back to face Brooklyn, saying, "I said that..." Then she quickly typed a few words and looked back at Brooklyn. "...to the Lord," she said in an abrasive old southern tone, and Brooklyn laughed at her mother, gave her a confused look, and shook her head.

Brooklyn went to her room, layed out across her bed, and called Cali, and after a few rings, Cali answered. "What's up wit' AK acting all retarded tho, girl?" Brooklyn sat the pillows up on her bed so she could lay back and talk. "I don't know what his problem is, but I wish he would quit being so petty. I already told him I don't want him." Cali got a call from her aunt and yelled out that she was coming.

"Well, you need to tell him again before somebody gets hurt. I'll hit you back, girl." she replied and then they said their goodbyes and hung up.

Brooklyn picked up the remote for her TV and started going through the channels until she saw one of her all-time favorite movies from when she was little. "Purple Rain." She turned it on, put the remote down, picked up her phone, and started scrolling through Instagram.

"Brooke, you got nail polish remover in there?" her mom yelled from the living room. "Yeah, here I come," she replied. She jumped up, walked to her dresser, and grabbed the tiny bottle. She took it over to her mother and handed it to her.

"Nothing less than a queen, right?" Nikki shouted. "Yes, Mother, nothing less than a queen," she shouted back the motto she and her mother shared. That was their little reminder to never be treated like anything less than a queen at all times.

The next day, Brooklyn and her crew were at the benches in front of the Rec Center, waiting for Kaleena the dance teacher to show up. Camisha was in the middle of a story about her cousin's boyfriend, who had taken the rent money her cousin had given him to pay the rent but instead tried to flip it and ended up losing all of it. Now, the both of them had nowhere to live, and she was asking her mother if they could stay with her. "Oh, hell to the nah," Cali shouted to the sky.

"What I look like, taking care of a man that can't take care of me? See, I'm trying to go here," Brooklyn said in all seriousness, holding one hand up above her head. "And if the nigga is down here somewhere," she held her other hand down by her chest, "then how is a bitch supposed to reach my full potential if I gotta keep going down here for you? What the fuck? That shit don't make no damn sense. I'll be damn If I let a nigga sidetrack me with his dumb shit," she shouted, with the rest of the girls in agreement.

"Cali, being Cali, always found a way to make a song out of anything somebody said to see if she could make it catchy enough to sound like the real hook of a song.

"I will never ever, never ever, ever never"

"Fuck off all my chedder, never ever, ever never"

"I mean that nigga better, better better better"

"Have his shit together, cause I'll never let a nigga side track a bitch..Ayye"

"Side track a bitch.. Ayye..side track a bitch.. Ayye"

"Side track a bitch.. Ayye..side track a bitch.. Ayye"

Cali sang her new chorus, as the rest of the girls joined in. Cali could get really animated sometimes. She had that way of making everybody around her have fun. "For real tho," she said as sort of an exclamation point after all the shenanigans were over.

"Hey, did y'all hear about the Chicago's Got Talent showcase at Mr. G's? I heard they gone have celebrity judges, and I think BET gone

63

be there. You better get up in that shit, bitch. I think you still got time to sign up," Vanessa told Cali before her ride pulled up. "Aye, hit me later and let me know if y'all come up with a song for the spotlight." She opened the door and jumped inside a black-on-black, 2017 Dodge Charger driven by lord knows who and sped off, bumping that new Lil Durk "Spin the Block" from that Signed to the Streets 3.

Once all the girls split up, Brooklyn went with Cali to her house to hang out while Cali grabbed her stuff so that she could go spend the night with Brooklyn. Cali's bedroom was the complete opposite of Brooklyn's. Cali didn't have teddy bears or pink stuff or any girlie stuff like Brooklyn did. Cali's room used to be her brother's and had all of his old DJ equipment, his milk crates filled with records, random wires, and pieces of things that went somewhere. She had an old MPC 2000 in the corner and his ASR 10 keyboard, and all his old posters covered her walls. She had Outkast, Tupac, Wu-Tang Clan, Jay Z, and the Crucial Conflict "Good Side/Bad Side" promo poster that had WildStyle with his back turned, throwing up the two C's.

She had a bunch of his old clothes that she would sometimes wear and a bunch of folders he had written everything down in, plus she had a bunch of her own folders that contained all of her raps from over the years all strewn about the surfaces of the room.

Cali's brother's death threw off the dynamics of the household, and the energy was never the same again. Anybody who knew Cali knew that she loved her brother and was still grieving and probably would continue for a long time. She still got teary-eyed every time she passed by a Guitar Center, remembering all the field trips she took with him there to buy new equipment. It had always been his dream to make it big in the music industry as a producer and music mogul, and since he would never see the dream come to fruition, Cali had it in her head that she would carry that dream on herself.

She finally gathered her things and threw them in her book bag, and then they went and hung out with her aunties for a minute before they left. Brooklyn liked hanging out with Cali's aunts; they were hilarious and ghetto, not the boujee type of ghetto like Nikki, but ghetto ghetto. Cali had Psyke and Maine come pick them up and drop them off. That's when they learned that it was not over between AK and Ledarius.

9.

Tick

You looking for Somebody?" - Brooklyn

When Ledarius walked through the door of the Rec Center the next morning, he got a funny feeling in his chest, as if his heart had skipped a beat. He was thinking about Brooklyn and her waistline, which reminded him of Jasmine, the Disney princess from the movie Alladin.

Ledarius was 16-years-old, and up to this point in his life, he had never been with a girl and definitely had never actually had sex yet. One time though, a few summers back, he had gotten something like a hand job from a girl named Keira, that lived over on Wolcott, but besides that, nothing.

He slowed down his pace as he approached the door to where Brooklyn's dance class was held so he could look inside without stopping, but when he didn't see anyone, he stopped, slightly hesitant, and peaked inside.

"You looking for somebody?" a soft, alluring voice said from directly behind him. He turned around, and there she was. His heart felt like a tiny explosion had gone off inside his chest, and his face suddenly warmed. "Oh...I...was...was...was just..." Ledarius nervously uttered. "Ah...Ah...Ah," she teased and looked at him with that tiny spark in her eyes and interrupted him. "You what? Your class is over there." She shot her eyes at the door behind him.

Brooklyn looked at him, noticed his shyness, and thought it was kind of cute in a way. Then she noticed how cute he really was, and she softened her tone a bit, shaking his hand. "I'm Brooklyn." She looked at him again and smiled.

"And I am Ledarius," he said gently, trying to avoid direct eye contact.

"Where you from, Ledarius?" she asked while she quickly looked him up and down.

"I am from 87th Street," he replied, still a little nervous but starting to get a hold of himself. Just then, Cali and the rest of the girls walked around the corner, but not too far behind them was AK and his boys.

When they walked up, the tension went up to ten instantly, and everybody felt it. Ledarius used his peripheral vision to count everyone coming up behind him without actually turning around. AK was tall and built like an NFL wide receiver. He had long dreadlocks, dark menacing eyes, and the aura of somebody who was truly dangerous. And now he was standing right behind him.

"What we doing over here, y'all? Congregating?" Tick said, walking up with AK and the rest of the homies. He stood in front of Ledarius and looked him up and down. "So, aye look, right?" Tick said, looking straight at Ledarius. "So, they say…that you…" he paused, took a toothpick out of his mouth and pointed at Ledarius, "was Master Yang's finest pupil and most fearless warrior." he continued. The whole room fell silent amidst a few chuckles from Maine and Psyke.

"I wanna test that," AK said, speaking for the first time and looking at Ledarius like he was waiting for him to say something. All eyes were on Ledarius, and the tension in the room had rose again. "My brethren here…would like to test that shit," Tick said, looking at Ledarius with a threatening undertone in his voice as everyone waited for what was about to happen next. Dajon walked up and stood behind Ledarius as if he could really have his back.

"I do not wish to fight you," Ledarius finally replied.

"I do not wish to fight you," Maine said in a little girlie voice, mocking the way Ledarius had just spoken. "Then who do you wish to fight?" AK said, staring Ledarius straight in the face. "Look, my guy," Tick leaned in, whispering to Ledarius as if he was trying to share some precious information with him, "if you don't fight…trust me, you don't wanna be what that makes you."

"Is choosing when to fight not the way of the wise?" Ledarius stood firm and wasn't about to fall for Tick and AK's attempts to intimidate him.

"Well, not being a little bitch ass nigga is the way of the wise around here, feel me?" AK said, standing there with his arms folded, looking at Ledarius like he couldn't wait to get his hands on him.

"Ole, talk like he in a bad Kung Fu flick-looking ass little boy," Psyke said, and Maine co-signed with a chuckle.

"Who this little nigga think he is?" Maine added.

"Man, that's Jet Li Darius," Jacob shouted from the crowd of people who had gathered around.

"Jet Li Darius...Jet Li Darius?" Tick screamed, and Psyke and Maine laughed out loud. "What the fuck did you just call this nigga boy?" He looked Ledarius up and down once more, covered his mouth, and laughed a couple more times. "He used to go to Master Yang's school back in the day, but he quit a little before y'all got here," Jacob explained and then he looked at Ledarius curiously and said, "Why did you quit?"

"I dont give a fuck why he quit," AK interjected before Ledarius could answer. "I wanna know how Master Yang let a coward that's too scared to fight me into the Dojo." He looked at Ledarius and stood up tall, showing how much bigger and stronger he was than him.

"Is it not the mark of a coward to attack the unwilling participant when he clearly has the advantage?" Ledarius replied.

"I know this nigga just didn't," AK said, sounding offended. "Boy, we in the jungle, either you're the predator or you the prey." Then, almost faster than a blinking eye, AK threw a super-quick punch towards Ledarius and stopped just a hair away from hitting him in the face, and when Ledarius didn't even so much as blink an eye, everybody who was watching started shouting in an uproar. "*Oooh,* he didn't even flinch," somebody in the back said.

AK didn't like that, which meant things might go left at any second, and what added fuel to that fire was the fact that Brooklyn was right there watching the whole thing. When a quick-thinking Dajon saw Master Yang coming up the hallway, he said, "Master Yang, can you settle a debate for us? Who was better, Bruce Lee or Jet Li?" Master Yang walked up and looked at everyone and gracefully bent down to Dajon's level and said, "Who do you think?" Then, everyone began to chatter in agreement and disbursed to their respective classes.

"That's what I said," Dajon said shaking his head and then he turned to go where he was supposed to be. Now, the whole place was buzzing with gossip. Who would win a fight between Ledarius and AK? That was the million-dollar question, and everybody was talking about it. It was even rumored that Dajon was collecting bets and planning to have t-shirts printed up with pictures of Ledarius and AK facing each other, looking really hard like a real Pay Per View fight promo flyer.

After an awkward class of energy jousting with AK and his goons, Ledarius finished putting up the equipment and cleaning up after everyone was gone. He wasn't going to tell Master Yang what was going on, so he pretended that everything was normal. On his way out, he saw AK and his friends in the parking lot hanging out next to the mothership, playing G Herbo's new mixtape.

Ledarius looked straight ahead, and just at the right time, he quickly walked out and tried not to be noticed. He got to the bus stop just as it was pulling up, jumped on, and sat down. When he got home,

Cynthia told him to go to the grocery store and get some milk, a pack of Newport 100's in a box, and two lottery tickets for his grandmother and take it over to her.

He went to the store, got everything his grandmother needed, and headed to the register. "Yo', where yo' brother at?" Nathan, who has worked behind the counter forever asked. "It's always cool to have Chicago's very own bootleg Boondocks Huey and Riley come in for a visit." He laughed to himself trying to be funny while Ledarius waited for him to be done amusing himself with the same joke that had grown tired long ago. Ledarius picked up his bag, collected his change, looked at the wannabe comedian, and left, heading towards his grandmother's house.

Once he dropped the groceries off, Ledarius turned around and headed to the probation office to check in with his PO. Once he arrived, he signed in, sat down and waited until his name was called. The beat-up old television that was holding on for dear life was showing the movie Friday. It was on the part where Smokey was trying to convince Craig that it would be a good idea if he got high today. "Craig, I'mma get you high, 'cause you ain't gotta go to work, and you ain't got shit to do," said the iconic character played by Chris Tucker.

Ledarius watched the movie until a short cocky dude in a tight polo shirt and khaki pants came out and called his name, then motioned for Ledarius to follow him. He got up and walked behind him until he reached an empty office and was told to sit down and wait. His probation officer was named Mrs. Thomas. She was a tall, slim woman of around 30-years-old with big brown eyes and a wide mouth. She had a hardened look on her face, but once she saw Ledarius, she lightened up and smiled.

"Hello, Ledarius. I am Mrs. Thomas, and I'm going to be your probation officer for the next six months. Have you signed up for your community service yet?" she asked Ledarius with a look of concern.

"Yes ma'am." He looked around her office, noticing all her certifications and acknowledgments. "Have you been arrested or have had any run-ins with law enforcement?" Mrs. Thomas asked.

"No, I haven't," Ledarius responded. She reached into her drawer, pulled out a silver bag, opened it up, pulled out a cup, and sat it on the table with a loud clang when it hit the wooden desk.

"Fill this up," Mrs. Thomas said as if it were just another day at the office.

"All the way?" Ledarius asked, wondering if he could produce enough urine to fill up the entire cup.

"Up to this line," she told him and got up to take him to the bathroom. He went in, unzipped his pants, and then he filled the cup up to the line. He walked back out of the bathroom, and she instructed him to put the cup on the counter. He placed the top on it, and she put a tape strip over the cap to seal it. Then, she escorted him back to her office to complete her paperwork.

"Okay, come see me next month on this date." She pointed to the sheet, and he stood up to leave, but before he walked out, she said, "And no fighting." Ledarius said, okay and wasn't too confident that he would be able to complete his probation without getting into any trouble considering what AK had just pulled the other day. He left the probation office and headed back home.

10.

Kaos

"Bitch, is you gone and lost your mind" - Kaos

"**F**uck Spike Lee, that damn *Chi-Raq* movie was some bullshit. The fuck was that nigga on?, Joe" Quan said as everybody weighed in with their own thoughts on how much they felt like that was, in fact, some real bullshit.

"Yeah, Spike Lee was a clown for that one, for real," Stimey agreed. Quan was searching for his lighter, which Gigi had to tell him he had right there next to him.

"Oh shit," he said and picked up the lighter and lit the blunt. "See, Spike Lee is a New York nigga, so he needs to stick to making New York movies. The fuck? See, the Black Panther nigga, Ryan Coogler, he's a Oakland nigga, and that's why he sticks to making Oakland movies."

"Nah, *Black Panther* was about Wakanda," Gigi giggled. "Them niggas was from Oakland, and what's his name? John Singleton, he an

LA dude. That's why he be making LA movies. Spike Lee old funny face ass need to stick to his own ghat damn geography." Quan spit a piece of something out of his mouth off the porch and hit the blunt.

"Yeah, I fucks with John Singleton. He made a bunch of classic ass shit, like muthafucking *Boyz n the Hood*, *Poetic Justice*, and *Hustle & Flow*," June said, adding his two cents. "Baby Boy to now, that's my shit," Gigi added. "Evette, I lie to you because I respect your feelings. If I told you the truth, that would mean I don't give a fuck," Quan said in a raspy voice, impersonating Tyrese Gibson's character Jody, and everyone started cracking up laughing.

"Jody, did you fuck Pandora?" Gigi said, playing like she was Taraji P Henson's character Evette. "Well, if you want me to…then I did," Quan responded in his Jody voice, and everybody laughed again. "Ya'll know what's good tho? That show *Snowfall* he got out, man that shit Gangsta." Uncle June commented as he struggled to get his lighter lit for his Newport. "Yo', what about that show *Power* tho, that dat boy 50 got out? That's my nigga right there." Quan hit his blunt and blew the smoke out before he finished.

"50 a muthafuckin savage. That nigga diss yo ass and end a nigga whole career, like fuck you niggas talking 'bout?" Quan stood up and puffed his chest out like he didn't weigh only a hundred fourteen pounds. "You know who the first one was to do that, don't you?" Uncle June said, forever being the local neighborhood hip-hop historian who claimed to even remember when R Kelly used to sing "A Change Gone Come" on the El platform back in the day. "KRS One, he was the first rapper to diss a nigga and end a nigga's whole career," he added and then he went into a few bars of KRS's song "The Bridge is Over" from his first album *Criminal Minded* proving his point.

Meanwhile, way across town, in "crazy nigga in his feelings news," Quan's boy Kaos, was in one of the trap houses screaming like a maniac on the phone with his baby momma, who recently took his son and moved with him to Memphis and was now living in the crib with some random dude.

"Bitch, is you gone and lost your muthafucking mind hoe?" he shouted into the phone. "Bitch is you possessed by evil spirits? You demon bitch you." Kaos screamed at the top of his lungs, yelling into his cell phone and squeezing it so tight that, in his mind, he was about to break it with his bare hands.

"We just fucked on Saturday bitch, now how many days later? Yo' cum bucket ass is out there doing dicks? Is that what the fuck you couldn't wait to go do, bitch? Huh? Bitch, it's Thursday," he continued to scream, and then he began to go through a wide range of emotions in a short period of time.

"Baby, I love you so much. You know you mean the whole world to me baby. Let's make it work. I'll quit hustling and get a real job. I'll quit doing everything you want me to do and be the man you need me to be, baby," Kaos said in his most sincere voice, about to cry, and then, in just a split second, on some bipolar as fuck shit, he completely snapped and flew into a full fit of rage. "Bitch, I'm coming down there right now to kill you, and him," he roared, and hung up the phone.

Now, Kaos only took what he needed to get there, get a room for a few days, and get back to Chicago, but the story now was that it was fifty thousand missing, and now Quan was on the chopping block with Moochie because of it. Kaos got his things together, grabbed his pistol and an extra clip, and got a Greyhound bus ticket on the first thing smoking outta Chicago. He caught the Greyhound at 95th with nothing but five hundred dollars, six cigarettes, a few pills, a cell phone charger, the blick, and a blunt and half of the one he smoked before he got on the phone. After that, he headed to Memphis, which was pretty risky considering that those Memphis niggas will kill you and keep going on about their day.

Ledarius walked up to his grandmother's house to the familiar scene of Quan and his crew sitting on the front porch, smoking and talking shit. They had all grown up on the front porches of the houses in this neighborhood. Some of the families living on this block had been in their homes for generations, and the older ones on the block had grown up the same way decades before.

Ledarius and DeQuan, as well as Stimey and Gigi, were the children of the children who had grown up here before them. Back then, the violence wasn't as out of control as it is today. Don't get me wrong; it's always been crazy, but not like it is today.

Ledarius, for the most part, stayed out of trouble because his main focus in life was martial arts. Quan, on the other hand, was a whole other story. He grew up in the streets, and just like so many others, he didn't see much of a life outside of the streets for him. He jumped off the porch early, as they say, and never looked back.

"What's up, Jet Ledarius?" one of the kids hanging out on the porch shouted when Ledarius walked up. Ledarius greeted everybody and headed inside to check on his grandmother. "What's up bruh?" Quan said, giving Ledarius dap when he got to the top of the stairs and opened the screen door to go inside.

"Grandma," Ledarius yelled and walked back towards the kitchen. She called out to him. She was in the kitchen peeling potatoes and talking on the phone. When he made it back there, she kissed him on the cheek and continued with her cooking, he gave her a hug. He then grabbed a banana from the bowl of fruit on the kitchen table and turned to leave.

On his way out, Quan and the gang were going back and forth about who was a better comedian, Dave Chappelle, Katt Williams or Kevin Hart. "Chris Rock is that nigga too now, let's not forget," Uncle June added, and then he went into how you can't forget about Mike Epps because he's a real nigga from Nap Town. "Fuck it then. Deray Davis, ghatdammit. Chi-Town in this bitch," Quan yelled out.

Ledarius slid by everyone, and before you knew it, he was gone. When he got home, Cynthia was watching YouTube videos on her phone and laughing. "That Jess Hilarious is stupid." Ledarius took some food out of the fridge, threw it in the toaster oven and then he went into the bathroom, washed his face. Once he was done, he looked at himself in the mirror. He dried his face off and went back into the kitchen to get his food while running the day's events back in his mind.

He took his food to his room and ate it on his bed. Suddenly, Brooklyn's face popped into his head, and her smile sent shock waves through his chest. Then, his thoughts got hijacked by the situation he was in with AK; and instantly wondered what he could do to make the whole situation go away. The last thing he needed was a probation violation.

11.

Nikki

"Lord, please don't tell me we live in a world where a boy
can be judged for loving his momma"   - Nikki

Nicole Yarbrow was a foster kid from Houston who grew up around the 5th Ward section of town. She was a combination of street-smart and book smart. Being sharp and pretty with the body of a comic book superheroine gave her an advantage in life. In every situation, she was always strategizing and coming up with the most pragmatic course of action.

Nicole and a friend of hers from foster care named Rachel hooked up and got an apartment together on the south side of Houston. Nicole went to school during the day and went to work at night. She always made the Dean's List and was all set to transfer her credits to a major university. One night, she came home from work, and Rachel's jealous boyfriend had lost his mind. He nearly beat Rachel too death in a fit of rage in their apartment. Soon after that, the girls moved out, and Nicole had to relocate.

Nicole had already spoken to the pastor at her church about the rooms he had for rent in case anything ever happened, and she needed to move. She grabbed what belongings she had and accepted the first college invitation that came her way. A short time later, she was on a train to Lafayette, Indiana, to attend Purdue University and never looked back.

While at Purdue, she met a young engineering major from the east coast and fell in what she thought was love. Matthew was from Rochester, New York, but had spent time in Brooklyn with family when he was younger. He used to tell people that he was related to Jay-Z because they shared the same last name, but that was a lie. Matthew was a small-time weed dealer on campus and had a way with the ladies, and Nicole was no different.

Nikki and Matt became the popular couple, and with her being good at math and economics, she helped him grow his marijuana business to where he was actually seeing real profits. The two were about to graduate, and they both had bright futures ahead of them.

Nicole graduated magna cum laude with her Delta sisters by her side. She was offered a job opportunity at a prestigious accounting firm in Chicago with a recommendation from her professor and moved into an apartment in Hyde Park. She soon found out she was pregnant and later gave birth to a baby girl who was 5 lbs. and 7oz. and Matthew named her Brooklyn.

Shortly afterwards, Nicole found out that Matt had two other children from two other girls they had attended school with. Nicole even remembered meeting one of the girls before when he introduced her to Nicole as his cousin. A while later, Nicole had closed on a house on the south side, packed her things, grabbed her daughter, and never looked back. Since then, she moved up in her company and, through a few smart financial investments, built a very comfortable life for herself and Brooklyn.

"Momma, how much wine did you have?" Brooklyn asked playfully as she sat down next to her mother.

"I've had the proper amount for a lady," Nicole answered in her fake English accent, which she used sometimes when she was feeling silly.

"Yeah, and how much exactly was that?" Brooklyn asked in a playfully angry tone. "However damn much a lady feels like," Nikki snapped back in her ghetto voice. They both laughed and then she took another sip of her wine.

"See, there is this new boy at the Rec, and I kinda think I might sorta like him, but I don't know if he my type though," Brooklyn said to her mom, waiting for her to respond so she could finish. "What's wrong with him? Do he got a lazy eye? I dated a boy in college once that had a lazy eye. They used to call that nigga Lazy Eye... Yep, he was cute and all, but I just couldn't see past that lazy eye." Nikki looked as if she was having a moment of reflection, and then she took a sip from her wine glass and snapped out of it.

"Momma, quit playing. I'm serious, or I'mma cut you off," Brooklyn said, annoyed, trying to reach for her mom's wine glass, but Nikki grabbed it first.

"Cut me off? No, no, no, honey, I cut you off," Nicole responded. "Just like I did when I cut you off my umbilical cord. That's right, I cut that shit myself 'cause I'm an independent Black woman, ghatdammit. Hell, they were taking too long, so I pulled out my own damn knife and went down there and said, 'Get this little *heffa* off of me.'" Nicole shot back and started making motions as if she were cutting her own imaginary umbilical cord.

Brooklyn started cracking up, and Nicole kept on cutting her imaginary umbilical cord with her imaginary knife until she was laughing too. "Okay, now tell me about your little cockeyed boy," Nicole asked.

"Momma, he not cockeyed. Pay attention. He's really cute, but he's like a momma's boy or kinda nerdy, I guess. I don't know. He's in the Karate class I told you about," Brooklyn said nervously.

"Lord, please tell me why we live in a world where a boy can be judged for loving his momma." She shook her head. "And girl, ain't nothing wrong with nerdy. You know who else was nerdy? Steve Jobs and Mark Zuckerberg. And look at 'em now—billionaires. These little boys with their pants hanging off they asses and out here living that street life, baby, most of them probably ain't gone make it. And let me tell you something else, they will keep you from making it too."

"The fastest way to poverty is getting pregnant by a loser, and it's plenty of them out here too, trying to shoot they're shot. It's up to you to dodge they ass like Neo baby." Nikki held her hands up, leaned back, and moved around in slow motion like Keanu Reeves in The Matrix. "Yeah, and if you get knocked up by one of them, believe me, the sequels just keep getting worse and worse."

"See, dumb niggas equal dumb shit. Let me put you up on the game." Nikki situated herself as if she had something top secret to share. "See, what comes out of a nigga's mouth is a direct reflection of what goes on in his head, and what goes on in a nigga's head directly determines his actions, so you gotta start right there with how dumb does this nigga sound when he talks and then move accordingly."

"Now, a smart man is going to do smart shit; like work, pay bills, go to church, save money, buy a house, invest in stocks, or start his own company. That's what you want honey. You can't make it nowhere in life with a dumb man 'cause all he's going to do is stop you from going anywhere because he'll think that if you start to rise, you will leave his dumb ass. And if he gets you pregnant, trust me, baby, it ain't worth it. My girlfriend back in Houston had a dumb nigga, and that dumb nigga almost killed her," Nikki said, looking directly at Brooklyn to drive her point home.

"Well, as long as he treats you like nothing less than a queen and keeps his hands to himself, we're good, 'cause a Forty-Five will put an end to all that Kung Fu shit real quick. You feel me?" Nikki smiled and held up her hand as if it were a gun. Brooklyn thought about what her mom had just told her, and the logic in it started to make sense to her. It was in that moment she knew Ledarius would be hers.

12.

Cali

"You might as well go make a reservation at Cook County" - Dajon

L edarius woke up early and went up to the roof to stretch and meditate. The sunrise was a bright golden cascade of sun rays to the east. The air was fresh, and the sky was filled with birds talking their shit early in the morning. Ledarius couldn't stop thinking about Brooklyn. That level of focus could only be achieved by the most disciplined, which he was not, because Brooklyn had his head gone, and there was nothing he could do about it.

He arrived at the Rec Center and was immediately stopped by Marcus. "Oh, guess who's back? I see you out here in the trenches, boy." He gave Ledarius some dap and told him to straighten up the magazines in the TV area before Master Yang got there.

Ledarius sat down and started looking through the magazines. One had Mayor Rahm Emanuel on the cover, which read the city was calling for his resignation for the lack of success in dealing with crime in the city, and another had a picture of Beyonce on the cover. Then, the magazine was suddenly ripped from his hand.

It was Brooklyn, and she looked like a music video should have been formed around her. Ledarius couldn't describe what she smelled like, but he knew that it must've been what heaven smelled like. She flipped through some of the pages and looked at him with her eyes. Then she smiled at him, and his heart melted like Taco Bell, Nacho Bell Grande cheese.

"Hey, don't let them get to you, okay?" she said, offering him his magazine back. "I was not planning on it," Ledarius replied. She was about to say something else when Cali and the rest of the girls strolled up and sat down. They spoke and quickly occupied themselves with magazines to fake giving Brooklyn some privacy.

Dajon came into the TV room and sat with the girls like a pimp from a 1970's Black exploitation film. Brooklyn wasn't sure the first time she met Ledarius, but she was pretty sure she liked him now. Then, AK and the boys walked up. "Brooklyn, come here for a minute," Tick asked her while the boys filed in around him.

"Boy, who you telling to come here, like what? I'm not one of yo' little breezys." Brooklyn smacked her lips and continued talking to Ledarius when AK approached. "My bad, he ain't mean to interrupt you over here acting like a hot little thot." He walked up to Brooklyn and stood in her face. "Boy, you better quit playing with me, Andre," Brooklyn expressed, standing her ground against him despite him being three times her size.

"She said she does not want you in her face. I think you should move." Ledarius said, looking him in the eyes for the first time.

"And who gone make me nigga? You?" AK asked, looking at Ledarius like he was ready for him to say one more thing so he could take all of his hostility out on him.

"Nah nigga… Me." Cali jumped off the table and ran up to AK with the rest of the girls behind her. "If you don't get yo' fake bootleg Black Dragon Ball Z looking ass the fuck out of my homegirl's face right now, you gon' have a real problem." The rest of the girls ran up behind her looking like they were ready to jump. "Move around nigga," she shouted and stood there with the meanest look on her face.

AK looked at Cali and decided that fighting a pack of girls wasn't in the plans, so he backed off and signaled Tick to come on. Then he looked at Ledarius and shook his head, turned around and walked off.

"These niggas must really be smoking on that stupid!" Cali assumed, looking around at the girls. "The fuck?" Cali, Brooklyn and the girls slowly began to disperse and head for dance class. Brooklyn turned towards Ledarius, but he was gone. She looked around, then turned and left with her friends.

"You might as well call ahead and see if you can make a reservation for a hospital room at Cook County Medical because AK is going to fuck you up," Dajon warned Ledarius as they headed for the gym. "See, I told you to stay off the radar, but you didn't listen. Now, not only are you all over the radar, but there's also arrows on the radar, and they all point towards you. Now, radars don't even have arrows, so that's how much you fucked up, arrows on radars, how do a nigga manage that?" Dajon continued talking as they walked down the hallway, shaking his head.

Later that evening, Brooklyn and Cali went to Brooklyn's house. Brooklyn went to her room while Cali went and hung out with Nikki. Nikki was more than just the cool mom. She treated Cali like she was her own. A few years ago, after her father and uncle were killed, she came to stay with them. They formed their own bond when Cali would wake up in the middle of the night after having nightmares, she would be sweating and talking to herself. While Brooklyn would still be asleep completely unbothered, Nikki and Cali would sit up and talk. Cali would cry, and Nikki would hold her and pray over her.

They had a bond that Brooklyn wasn't exactly aware of, and that's why Nikki was the only person who could actually get Cali to dance. "Come on, girl, let me show you how we used to get down back in my day." She put on the 90's classic "Anything" by SWV and Coco set out to remind bitches who really ran the 90's.

Nikki and Cali jumped in front of the living room mirror in their socks and busted out a full-on 90's medley of seemingly choreographed dance routines. Brooklyn came out of her room and stared at her mother and her best friend doing a full-on show right there in the living room. It didn't take long for her to jump in there and make their dance group a trio. Brooklyn's natural talent and her need for the spotlight soon had her leading the dance routines with Nikki and Cali on each side of her keeping up.

Cali didn't drink, but she had a few sips of wine and decided to confess to Nikki that when they were younger, and the three of them would have movie nights, she and Brooklyn would always finish off Nikki's wine bottles after she fell asleep. Once, they finished a whole bottle, got drunk, and had headaches the rest of the weekend. The three of them hung out just like old times, talking long into the night about any and everything until they all eventually tired out and turned in to get some sleep.

13.

AK

"You tough now" - AK

Andre Kennedy was the type of dude who'd root for the bad guy in the movie. He hadn't even seen his 18th birthday yet and was already 6 feet tall and strong like a professional athlete. He had long locks and was covered in tattoos.

He and his brethren, as they sometimes would refer to themselves, always wore black and red, and everything had their symbol on it, which resembled a little red fireball but more sinister. Even AK's truck, a black and red chromed-out custom Cadillac Escalade, had their symbol on the doors and in various other spots.

AK moved to the neighborhood from somewhere in the 100's when he was 12-years-old to live with his aunt. When he got to the neighborhood, it was said that he had suffered some sort of traumatic experience and hadn't spoken in months. The neighborhood kids showed him no mercy and teased him every chance they got. They even came up with the theory that he was a little slow.

When Andre was 10, his father was killed by a family friend over some money he had borrowed but wasn't ready to pay back. Words got exchanged, and a fight ensued. AK was devastated after his father's murder and became more and more introverted. His father had served in the army but was kicked out with a dishonorable discharge for something to do with drugs. He never really wanted to talk about it.

AK grew up with a strict upbringing that only the kids of a military dad would understand. He started martial arts early and was highly skilled by the time he hit puberty. When he was young, he loved to play a game he made up called "Neighborhood Ninja," which was basically just him sneaking around the neighborhood, climbing trees and hiding in bushes.

AK read a lot of comic books growing up as a way to escape and keep his mind occupied. The heroes were always corny to him with their morals and self-righteous rhetoric. He always secretly wished that Magneto would defeat the X-Men or that Doctor Doom would finally get his wish and destroy the Fantastic Four.

His infatuation with evil villains, coupled with misplaced anger and the fact that he was a very formidable Karate student that was secretly obsessed with killing the person who murdered his father, gave Andre a mission in life.

One night, while out playing Neighborhood Ninja, he stumbled upon the truth about his father's murder and who was responsible. His father's best friend, whom Andre had called uncle since he was a kid had in fact killed him over 75 dollars. He heard him confess to his girlfriend on the phone one night while AK was outside his window in a full ninja suit, and something inside of him snapped.

A week later, they found his father's friend stabbed to death in his apartment, and the police had no suspects and ruled it a drug homicide because there was crack discovered at the scene. No one was ever caught, and the case remained unsolved to this day.

Afterward, something else began to eat away at Andre, something about what the police said the night his father was killed. Andre was in full gear the night his father was shot and was hiding in a tree above where his father's body was laid out on the sidewalk.

When the ambulance driver allowed the detectives to investigate the body, Andre overheard one of the police officers say, "This nigger probably got what was coming to him. Let's hurry this up and go toss back a couple." Andre was crushed, and that fueled the hatred that still burns inside of him to this day.

Devastated by the loss of her husband and now the unsolved killing of his friend, Andre's mother thought it would be best for him to leave and go stay with her sister for a while because she feared all the death and commotion would be too traumatizing for little Andre.

When he came to the block, he had not spoken a word in weeks and only communicated with subtle gestures and facial expressions. Being the weird new kid who couldn't talk, caused some kids to pick on him, and when he didn't defend himself, it continued as you might expect.

One day, while Andre was riding his bike down the alley, some kids were out playing with water guns, and when Andre rode by, they sprayed him in his face, and one of the boys kicked his back tire and made him crash head-on into some nearby trash cans.

After Andre picked himself up off the ground, he grabbed his bike, and one of the kids shouted, "You need to throw that old rusty piece of shit in one of those cans you just crashed into." All the other kids burst into laughter and started shooting their water guns at him. Andre was humiliated, but he didn't do anything, and that made the kids think he was scared. But he was more scared of what he would do to them and the consequences that would follow.

One 4th of July, some of the neighbors from the block went to the Forest Preserve to cook out and let off fireworks. It also happened to be close to the anniversary of his father's death. The parents and the kids had enough activities to keep them entertained all day. Andre came with the intention of eating all the barbecue he could, watching the fireworks and leaving.

While he was sipping on a Dr. Pepper and waiting for his second plate, the boys who had been harassing Andre popped up, and when he saw them, he decided it was time to go, but they followed. When he saw them following behind him, he took off running, and they ran behind him. Then, the kids who knew what was going on took off running behind them.

Andre headed for the tunnel that went underneath the street above it to get from the 86th Street side of the street over to the 87th Street side. He ran through the tunnel, and the boys and spectators followed them.

When he arrived on the 87th Street side, he turned around and hit the first boy in the face so hard that his body practically flipped over. He was knocked out before he even hit the ground. It almost looked like it was in slow motion.

Everybody that witnessed what had just happened froze like Lake Michigan in the dead of winter. The way his body hit the ground sent shock waves through everyone. Then Andre looked at the rest of the boys. "What's the matter, huh?" he walked towards them, and they backed up. "What's the matter, you scared? Come on, any one of you bitch ass niggas can get it." But none of them moved and their friend was laid out unconscious on the ground.

Andre walked up to the one who looked like he was the toughest out of the bunch, and knocked him to the ground. He then reached down and grabbed him by his shirt and snatched him back up to his feet. "What's up now?" He had a look in his eyes that they had never seen before, and everybody was looking like, "Oh shit, Andre hit him really fast, like four or five times knocking him to the ground again, but he didn't stop there. Andre kept hitting him until blood started gushing from his nose and face and asking him questions while he was beating him. "You tough now?" He roared as he pulverized the other boy's face. Then he stood up and asked if anybody else felt tough, which they all declined.

After that day, it was firmly established in the minds of everyone who witnessed what happened, knew that Andre was not to be fucked with. He had everybody intimidated except for one kid. Anthony Bell was there that day and witnessed the whole thing, and when AK looked for anyone else who wanted to step to him, he caught eyes with Anthony, and he nodded in approval. He wasn't scared because Anthony, who would later go by the name Lunatic, carried a snub nose .38 in his front pocket. It only had four bullets in it, but that was enough for him not to be worried about anybody coming for him. After that day, Tick and AK hooked up and had been tight like brothers ever since.

Tick had carried a pistol on him ever since his brother was killed due to gang violence a year before. After he and AK hooked up, it was over; nobody wanted that much smoke, and later, the rest of the squad filled out. Jermaine, also known as Maine, also known as Maniac, and Philip, who went by the name Psyke, which was short for Psycho, had become a dangerous collective. A couple of years later, they met Fang, a black and Korean-born martial arts prodigy.

They formed a bond, and later, they formed a gang. They called themselves The Brethren Assassin, which was short for The Brotherhood of Assassins, also known as the B.O.A or simply the Boa Boys, depending on who was telling the story. They began cracking cars and flipping the money into secret underground fight clubs among a wide array of whatever else they were rumored to be into. Those that knew about them knew not to get in their way because no matter how gangster a dude thought he was, what you don't want is a bunch of niggas that moved like ninjas on yo ass.

14.

The Boys

"Kryptonite Kills Superman" - Tick

"**M**agneto was right ghatdammit," AK shouted as the credits rolled at the end of the movie "*X-Men: First Class*," they'd just finished watching. He hit the blunt and held in the smoke as he looked around the room for support of his theory. "These muthafuckin humans are trying to kill us Charles," he managed to say before he blew the smoke out his mouth.

"And Professor X ass be like, 'Naw Eric, we gotta be peaceful with the humans. They know not what they do.'" AK eased into character. "Magneto was like, 'Fuck that shit Charles, and fuck you and fuck the X-Men, My nigga now what?'" Everybody started laughing, which only hyped him up.

"Oh, what? You finna go get Wolverine nigga? Oh, you finna go get Wolverine now, huh? You finna run and get Colossus and nem? Well, come on then ain't nobody scared of Gambit nigga. I get something for they ass Jack." Everybody started laughing, and AK stood up and hit the blunt again.

"Juggernaut, come over here, my dude, and run these niggas over right here. And Mystic, you come over here, ghatdammit, and turn into that guy probation officer right here. I betcha he gon' go home if he see his PO pull up." Everyone cracked up until Psyke brought up that he preferred DC over Marvel, and that sent AK into another tangent.

"Fuck Superman," he said and dumped the ashes from the blunt into the ashtray and looked up with a whole new look on his face as if he were changing into someone else. "Lex Luther out here jugging, doing what he do, minding his muthafucking bidness, and here come Superman bitch ass, flying all up on niggas wit' his bullshit, lame ass nigga." AK mocked, totally in character now.

"What are you doing now, Lex Luther?" AK inquired in an exaggerated news reporter's voice, imitating Superman.

"Minding my muthafucking business, Superman. Ghatdammit, move around man, damn. Why is you fucking with me?"

Maine agreed while he was finishing up rolling another blunt. "Superman be on that bullshit. Can you imagine that muthafucka flying up on the block? Walking around looking all through the trap house with X-Ray vision and shit." He started looking around the room like he had X-ray vision.

"With his looking ass," Tick chimed in. "Oh, I see you got some dope in there, fellas. I'mma have to come and fuck yo shit up now." They all laughed, and Maine lit the blunt he'd just finished rolling. "Superman ass need to worry about being there for his bitch," AK added.

"Go home to yo woman, Superman, and take her out to eat, take her dancing, women like that shit. Buy her flowers and spend some quality time with her instead of fucking with me every day," he hit the blunt and continued. "Lois Lane little fine ass walking around in that skirt. She ready, you already know what it is, she getting that check, ghatdammit. Jay Jonah Jameson gon' pay his people." AK paused to hit the blunt. "No, that's Spiderman. Jay Jonah Jameson is Spiderman's boss at the..." Maine started to say, but AK cut him off. "I don't give a fuck. She getting a check, ain't she?" He shouted, and then he paused for dramatic effect and said, "And Superman don't even appreciate it," and everybody burst out laughing. Ak blew smoke in the air and continued.

"Niggas don't care about you being bulletproof neither, Superman. Trust me, a nigga will figure out some way to get your ass up outta here," AK commented, holding a mean mug in place on his face.

"Kryptonite," Tick said. "Kryptonite kills Superman," he said again. AK turned around and looked at everybody, and Maine hit the Bluetooth speaker from his phone and turned on that Big Boi, Purple Ribbon record. *"I be on that Kryptonite straight up off that Kryptonite. I be on that...I be on it...I be on the Kryptonite,"* and everybody in the house started dancing and rapping along with the lyrics and blowing smoke out all over the room. Once the song was over, it was back to business, ass-beating business, and Ledarius was number one on the list. It was finally time to cross him off for good.

Meanwhile, DeQuan had been trying to call Kaos all day but had not gotten an answer. "Man, where the fuck is this nigga at Joe?" DeQuan shouted. Stimey walked up and shook hands with him. Then, he walked to the top of the stairs and sat an old gray book bag, he carried with him sometimes, in the corner of the porch, next to the front door. He came back and sat at the top of the stairs, pulled out a cigarillo, and started breaking up some weed.

DeQuan sat down and started rocking back and forth in a way that helped him internalize the utter rage he was feeling at the moment. He had a bad feeling, and his gut instincts usually had merit. He pulled out the half blunt he had and lit it. Then he pulled his phone out to check Kaos's Instagram to see if he could find some sort of clue as to where this nigga was. He knew that if he didn't turn up soon, eventually Moochie was gonna get wind of it, and that was what Quan didn't want.

Moochie was shirtless in his apartment with two women, a white girl and a black girl. They were smoking weed and bumping that Montana 300. The girls were snorting coke off a mirror and getting freaky with Moochie, and sometimes each other.

Moochie was a drug dealer with a violent history, and after assuming control of the empire started by DeQuan's father, his level of extravagance only grew. He was always strapped up and always had shooters nearby. He made a lot of money, and he blew it fast. Sex, drugs, and expensive shit were his forte'. He owned multiple apartments in his building and kept his security on a tight detail.

Outside in the front of his apartment was his right-hand man, Bruza. Bruza was arguing with another guy who was trying to compare

LeBron James to Michael Jordan and occasionally overseeing the guys that were out moving the work when two girls began to argue not far away from where he was posted.

"Hey, y'all gotta take that shit down the street and around the corner. What the fuck is wrong with you bitches? This ain't love and hip hop. Y'all fucking with my tranquility out here. Move around," he yelled. "Look, LeBron is great, I'll give him that, but that nigga complains too fucking much. Jordan didn't complain even when he played sick or hurt. He sucked that shit up and delivered, and Kobe was the same way. When things don't go LeBron's way, he come up with excuses and shit. He needs to be worried about Curry, and tell his fans to get off Jordan's dick," he explained as he saw one of the soldiers walk up.

"What up, Bruza?" Lil Troy spoke as he took his last pull and threw down the cigarette he was smoking. He was nervous, and Bruza, off the rip, could tell that something was wrong. "Man Joe, where Moochie at G?" He said, looking slightly uncomfortable. "He unavailable right now. You holla at me, what's good?" Bruza asked him.

"Yo', that boy Kaos den ran off," he explained as he shook his head back and forth. "What you mean he ran off?" Bruza asked in shock because he knew Moochie was going to go ballistic. "Yo' that nigga up outta here and some of the money and some of the work missing," he said. "What? Is you sure fam?, it is what you say it is?" Bruza added, hoping there was some sorta doubt in his mind. "I'm sure sure. The nigga was talking about going to kill a nigga over his baby momma."

"Fuck!" Bruza shouted. He thought about it for a second, took a deep breath, and told Lil Troy to stay downstairs and work the block. Bruza went up to Moochie's apartment and knocked on the door.

After a few minutes, the door flung open, and Moochie stood there in his boxer drawers and socks. "What up, Bruza? I thought I told you to hold my calls?" Moochie said, signaling Bruza to walk inside. The house was full of marijuana smoke and liquor cups, with the two girls on the couch kissing each other.

"Yo', that boy Kaos den got ghost," Bruza said in a low whisper. "What?" Moochie said. "Yeah, and he cuffed some of the bread and some of the work before he dipped," Bruza told him and explained everything Lil Troy had just told him. Moochie was furious, so he told Bruza to call Quan because Quan was the person who vouched for him. Bruza pulled out his phone and called DeQuan, but it went to voice mail.

"He ain't pick up. What you want me to do?" he asked him as he slid his phone back into his pocket. "Nothing yet. Let me deal with this. You make sure everything run squeaky around here. I might just have to get a little creative with this one," Moochie told him. He went back to the festivities taking place in the living room while Bruza let himself out. He knew Moochie and knew how he dealt with people that he thought stole from him. He went back downstairs with Lil Troy and told him to get back to the spot and keep his ear to the street because shit was about to hit the fan.

15.

The Last Dragon

"Bruce Leroy had a mission, find the master, reach the final level and achieve the golden glow, your ass just trying to get off probation" - DeQuan

The Brethren Assassins were all kicking it at AK's spot as usual, smoking and talking shit. Psyke had the remote control and was flipping through channels. "Yo' right there, Revolt TV, that's like the new MTV that nigga P Diddy got." Maine broke the blunt down and dumped the guts in the plastic bag he had just brought his snacks in.

"Yo', ok den, he den done enough for the culture that if he says this is the new MTV, and this what we watching from now on, then ghatdammit, this is what the fuck we watching from now on." AK hit the blunt, sat back in the chair, held his head up, and blew the smoke out in a big white cloud.

"Yo', guess what's coming on TV tonight brethren?" Psyke announced as he came in from picking up a box that UPS had just delivered. "Titanic?" Maine answered with enthusiasm. "No nigga! Why the fuck would I be walking in here talking 'bout some damn Titanic?" Psyke shot back. "'Cause it's a great movie," Maine replied sarcastically. "It won an Oscar," AK chimed in, fucking with Psyke. "Leonardo's performance was brilliant," Fang chimed in, joining in on the fun they were having at Psyke's expense. "Really tugs at the heartstrings," Tick said, continuing the barrage of sarcastic comments. "No, genius. *The Last Dragon* is coming on Bounce TV tonight," Psyke stated, hopefully putting an end to all the jokes.

Everybody looked as if they didn't know which movie he was talking about specifically. "The Last Dragon is the movie that that bitch ass nigga got the name Jet Ledarius from. Nigga, the dude in the movie is named Bruce Leroy. That's who the nigga trying to be like," Psyke explained to the rest of them, who supposedly had never seen it. Fang said he thought he might have seen it before, but he couldn't remember.

A few hours later, they were all smoking weed in AK's apartment and watching The Last Dragon on his 52-inch. "So, this that's nigga's shit, huh?" AK asked as if he didn't already know the answer to his own question. "This the movie the nigga based his whole swag on? That's why this muthafuckin' nigga so corny." He made a couple of strange faces, then he hit the blunt, leaned back in his chair, and stared at the television as the smoke rose in the air, adding a mysterious atmosphere to the room. When it was over, AK seemed galvanized.

"Man, Sho nuff really wanted to put hands on that Mark, Joe," Maine said after he hit the blunt and put it out, then stood up to go to the bathroom. "Yeah, he did, didn't he?" AK said as he pulled on his blunt one more time, and then suddenly, out of nowhere, a truly wicked look came over his face. Tick and Psyke looked over at AK and started calling his name, but he wouldn't answer. He just stared at the television as if he were a man possessed.   Meanwhile, across town Cali was staying over at Brooklyn's house. They were also watching the showing of The Last Dragon on Bounce TV. The girls were having a movie night just like old times with Nicole, who was sipping her wine and eating from a big bowl of fruit, and talking about how fine she and all her friends thought Bruce Leroy was back then, and how he could still get it. Brooklyn had never seen it, but Cali vaguely remembered her brother watching it before or talking about it or something.

Ledarius was at home with his mom and brother sitting on the couch in the living room in front of the TV, also watching The Last Dragon for the thousandth time with Quan walking in and out and talking his shit as usual. "Man Joe, I'm telling you, my nigga in this movie is this nigga right here. Eddie Arcadian, that crazy muthafucka be on his bullshit," Quan said, referring to the villain played by the actor Christopher Murney, as the fast-talking shyster who was trying to get Lara Charles, the love interest of Bruce Leroy, to spin his talentless girlfriend's record on her show.

"Everything that comes out that fool's mouth is straight comedy," Quan stated. "Watch...knock it off," Quan shouted the lines by heart. "Don't bug me, and fix your face," he shouted again, mimicking the pint-sized gangster shouting at the timid pop star with the colorful hair, and an even crazier stage costume that she walked around wearing even when she wasn't performing. "Shut up!" Quan yelled out again, right along with the actor on screen.

"Alright, Jet Ledarius," Quan said. "Let me breathe on you, grasshopper." He turned to Ledarius in all seriousness. "Now, don't you start trying to glow around this muthafucka, bro. You know niggas ain't about to let no niggas out here outshine them. They will shoot you for some shit like that, trying to glow, and you ain't got enough teeth to catch all them bullets. I'm just keeping it a buck," Quan added, ridiculing his brother for his own amusement. "Momma," Quan shouted, "tell Ledarius he better not start trying to glow."

"Hell nah, baby. You don't wanna do that," Cynthia joined in on the fun. "They don't like it when niggas start trying to glow and shit. Uh um, the last one that tried that, they shot him over there by Simeon under the viaduct. They was like, 'Nigga, is you glowing? Who told you you could glow over here? All hell nah, we ain't having niggas glowing around here, Joe.' They was like, 'Ayye....ayye, this nigga over here trying to glow, trying to glow around all the bitches, fuck that.' Then they shot him. Niggas ain't glowed around here since, baby." Cynthia finished her story as if it was actually factual. "Told you!" Quan agreed.

"Besides, Bruce Leroy had a mission; to find the master, reach the final level, and achieve the golden glow. Yo' ass is just trying to make it off probation," Quan said once again, amusing himself at his brother's expense. They finished watching their movie, and afterwards, when they went to their room, Ledarius couldn't get Brooklyn out of his mind. He stood in the mirror looking at himself, and then he decided he needed some advice about what he should do next.

"Quan, I would like to ask you something," Ledarius asked nervously. "Well shoot, 'cause I don't have all day to be dilly-dallying around here with you. My time is money, and it would be uncivilized for me to waste either one," Quan replied nonchalantly.

"Well, I want to know, how do you get a girl to like you?" he asked, expecting Quan to blow him off with some sort of slick comment. "Well...well...well, the boy is finally ready to be a man. I'm glad you came to me. I guess you really not as lame as you look. Who is she?" he asked, still surprised that they were even having this conversation.

"There is a girl at the Rec Center. Her name is Brooklyn, and she is very pretty," Ledarius said with a hint of excitement that was rare for him when talking about anything except martial arts.

"Well, first, you gotta stop being so lame. I mean, a girl doesn't want a dude that everybody laughs at. They want a boss, a real nigga, not nobody walking around all nerdy," he said.

"Double negative," Ledarius said.

"What?" Quan responded. "Not nobody is a double negative. Ledarius explained. "See, that's what I mean. Who cares?" Quan yelled. "You gotta quit being so weird all the time," he advised as he stood there looking at Ledarius, shaking his head.

Quan looked at his brother with a deep seriousness. "Dare, you not a virgin, are you?" he asked with a slight whisper in his voice as if someone else was around to hear him. Ledarius gave a nervous look. "You are, aint you? Wait, no you're not. You had Quiana. That girl was in love with you. Y'all spent every day together that summer, and you mean to tell me y'all didn't smash? Awww shit, Dare, what was y'all doing over there all that time? Exchanging beauty tips?" Quan joked and started laughing. "You ain't let her put no gel in your hair, did you, Darri? Aww hell nah, you did, didn't you? I can't believe you. Did you ever consider how your lameness was going to affect me? What's that thing the rich white kids do when they take their parents to court and divorce 'em and shit?" he asked, shaking his head.

"Emancipation," Ledarius replied.

"Hell yeah, I gotta get emancipated from you, man." He continued to laugh. "You got me out here looking lame by association, Ledarius," Quan said, looking slightly perplexed.

"Will you just help me now? This is serious," Ledarius asked.

"Okay, okay, I knew it was bound to happen one day. Look, you gotta talk to her, make her laugh, ya dig? And let her know you the boss," Quan explained.

"I am no boss. I don't even own a company," Ledarius said.

"I am no boss. I don't even own a company," Quan mocked Ledarius like he used to do when they were kids. "You gotta be cool, you gotta be smooth," he added. "I don't know how to be cool," Ledarius said sadly.

"Wow, I didn't know I had so much work to do. You sad, Joe, real sad."

"Well, just be yourself, bro. Maybe she'll take pity on you. Pity sex is just as good as any sex, and if you gon try to work that angle, then you gotta work that angle to the fullest, you feel me?" Quan said, trying his best to give his brother some game. "I'm not trying to work any angle," Ledarius replied, still not satisfied with the advice he was receiving. "Well, you better work something, Joe, or you gon be working your right hand for the rest of your life. Lotion and tissue can get real expensive if you ain't got a steady income. You better move fast 'cause she ain't gon wait around forever for you to figure it out," DeQuan warned as he reached up and turned off the lamp, leaving only the streetlights outside shining in through their bedroom window.

16.

World Star

"That boy softer than wet toilet paper" Tick

AK, Tick, and the crew were in a warehouse in Indiana, waiting for a guy named Bones to show up. "Now, after this lick, we'll have enough for the buy-in, and then once I take out that fool Enoch, I'll be the new king, and then we'll be able to get back control of the Coliseum." AK announced to his boys while they sat in the lobby of an oversized auto body shop.

"The Coliseum" is where the underground fighting league AK and the boys were a part of was held each and every week. A lot of powerful ballers from Chicago, Ohio, Indiana, Michigan, and St. Louis get together and hold tournaments for big money, kind of like the way the big-time hustlers do in New York with the basketball games at Rucker Park. AK and the boys had control of it for a while but got swindled out of it by the Panamanian family of his then-business partner Enoch. It had been his personal mission ever since to get it back under the control of the Brotherhood.

A man named Bones with unusually strong arms walked out wearing a sleeveless muscle shirt and signaled for AK to come over. "What you got for me, Dr. Dre?" Bones asked AK while holding on to the toothpick in his mouth.

Bones was the guy you went to when you considered cracking cars for a living and needed the most bang for your buck. Cracking cars was basically stealing a car and then changing the paperwork and making that stolen car legal.

"Three brand new top-of-the-line Maserati's," AK replied and signaled for his boys to open the large door and drive them onto the showroom floor. "Nice," Bones said, looking over the cars with the eye of an army sergeant doing inspections. "A'ight, Dr. Dre, let's go settle up. Leave the Scooby gang here," he insisted and started towards the backroom with AK right behind.

"Yo', I can't wait for the new episode of Drink Champs to come out this week. That nigga N.O.R.E is a damn fool," Psyke said. "Yeah, he be talking shit with that damn smirk on his face all the time, but, what we gon do about that little bitch ass nigga at the Rec?" Maine asked the guys while they sat waiting for AK to get back. "Let's World Star that pussy ass nigga so that everybody knows what'll happen to them when the Boa Boyz smell blood," Psyke stated, excited by the idea of beating him up and embarrassing Ledarius for the whole world to see. "Hell yeah," Fang agreed. "That boy softer than wet toilet paper." Tick added to the amusement of the others. AK came from the back with Bones and nodded his head to the guys that everything was taken care of.

"Yo', we need to World Star that lil punk ass Ledarius," Psyke told AK as if he just came up with the greatest idea since Facebook. "Yeah, I like that," AK acknowledged as they walked to the mothership, jumped in, and pulled off. "Yeah, I got something real special planned for that little bitch." AK told them as they headed towards the freeway back to the city. "Hell yeah," Tick and the boys agreed, and they lit up their blunts once they hit the freeway.

The Brethren had a policy in place where they were prohibited from getting high while handling any Brotherhood business, so a lot of the time, once business was finally done, then they lit up and smoked. "Yo', this is a new strand I'm developing. I call it Ginseng Pink Lemonade." Tick announced and then he hit it and savored the flavor of his new creation, blowing the smoke out of the sunroof as they sped up, bumping that Lil Bibby "You Ain't Gang."

17.

Damn Straight

I'm 'bout to beat your ass like it's report card day" - Damn Straight

Music filled the hallways of the Rec Center. Brooklyn and the girls had finally decided on the song for the spotlight dance-off. The old-school funk beat started bumping through the speakers and filled the room, and Brooklyn, the star of the show, was ready to do her thing. The song she had decided on was the extended dance version of the song "Sex Shooter," whose original version was recorded by Vanity 6, but was later re-recorded after she turned down her role in the film "Purple Rain", which went on to become hugely successful. Their exotic dance moves captivated everyone watching. The 80's funk beat was given a whole new life as they performed modern dance moves that would have made Prince himself grin from ear to ear.

When they got off stage, all the girls gathered around, giving them praise for the work they put into their routine. "Girl, you did that," they said, with everyone else agreeing and giving her hugs. Her dance teacher gave her a thumbs up and told her to keep the same energy for the show they were putting on in a couple of weeks. On their way out, they stopped by the front desk to talk to Marcus and Miss Freeman, who asked how everything went.

"Good, we got top billing for the 4th of July show," she explained to Miss Freeman. "How's my baby?" Brooklyn asked Marcus about his daughter Iyana who they all knew and loved because Marcus used to bring her with him to work sometimes. "She good, but still a handful and a half. I don't know where she gets her little diva attitude from," he responded and pulled out his phone to show the girls the most recent pictures of her.

"Oh my God, she is the cutest thing in the whole wide world," they all said, gushing over each picture.

"Bring her up here to the 4th of July show," Brooklyn begged.

"Okay, okay," Marcus agreed. Then the girls left and went to get food at the restaurant on the corner from the Rec.

Dajon was in front of the Rec rocking the Rajon Rondo New Orleans Pelicans Jersey, selling candy with Bug and another kid behind him that he was supposedly training to take over the business someday. "Jet Ledarius, what's happening with it?" He asked as he walked up and gave him a dap.

"What's up with you Dajon?" Ledarius asked.

"Man, posted like a thumb tac, trying to stay sucker free in a land full of lollipops, ya dig? Master Yang ain't here yet," he told him.

"Yeah, he wants me to get the class warmed up until he gets here. Why don't you come help me?" he asked Dajon, and they headed to the makeshift Dojo to get the equipment out. When they walked into the locker room, the door suddenly slammed shut behind them; it was AK and his gang of rogue assassins. "Oh shit, it's a set-up," Dajon screeched, appearing startled.

AK stepped in front of Ledarius with a menacing look on his face. "You ready to fight me yet, punk?" AK roared in a voice that was completely different from the way he usually spoke. Ledarius didn't know what to do. Fang and Psyke were blocking the door behind them, and Tick and Maine were standing on both sides of AK, who seemed bigger and more muscular now for some reason.

"AK, this is not the way," Ledarius said, trying to reason with him.

"Who is AK?" he replied once again in that menacing tone. "Nah, punk, from now on, my name is Damn Straight," he stated with a crazed look in his eyes. Ledarius didn't know what was happening, and he certainly didn't know how to respond, and then Damn Straight screamed.

"Am I the meanest?" And Tick, Fang, Maine, and Psyke shouted in unison, "Damn Straight!"

"Am I the prettiest?" They all shouted again, "Damn Straight!"

"Am I the *baddest* muthafucka low down around Chi-Town?" They all shouted again, "Damn Straight!"

Then he yelled again, "I can't hear you." And they shouted again, "Damn Straight!" Then he said, "*Yeeeah,*" with that same crazed look in his eyes, just like the antagonist Sho Nuff did in the movie "The Last Dragon," and walked up on Ledarius. "I'm the Sho Gun of Chi-Town now, and since you too much of a little bitch to fight me, then you might as well bow down right now to a real master," Damn Straight instructed Ledarius, looking like any second he was about to punch Ledarius in the face. "Bow down, bitch, and kiss these Jordan's, or you got an ass whooping with your name on it," Damn Straight threatened him. Ledarius couldn't believe what was happening. He would have thought that AK was joking, but the look on his face said he was serious.

"Kiss these Jordan's, Ledarius, and I don't mean no little peck neither, nigga. I better feel some emotion," AK said, looking as if he was literally getting stronger by the second. "You know what, AK? You are not yourself right now," Dajon stepped in. "See, that's a side effect of hunger. That's why you need to bite into this delicious Snickers bar and let all these tasty peanuts and caramel make all that aggression go away." Dajon said, trying to distract Damn Straight.

"Grab him," Damn Straight roared, and Psyke grabbed Dajon from behind and put him in a headlock. Now bow down, Jet Ledarius, and kiss these Jordan's bitch, or I'mma have Psyke snap his neck." Ledarius looked nervous momentarily then Dajon screamed. "If you snap my neck, my uncles gon come up here with them sticks tomorrow busting."

"Let him go," Damn Straight demanded, and Psyke quickly released Dajon, who looked pissed as he bent over and started picking his candy off the floor. "Get him outta here," AK ordered them, and they grabbed Dajon, threw him out of the locker room, and slammed the door. "We not finished with you yet, Ledarius," Damn Straight warned with the crazy look on his face becoming more intense.

"You got an ass whooping coming your way, Ledarius," Damn Straight shouted. "Yeah, you got an ass whopping coming like your momma just went up to the school to meet with your teacher, and you know you got fucked up grades in all your classes!" Damn Straight shouted once again. "THAT'S RIGHT LEDARIUS. I'M ABOUT TO BEAT YO ASS LIKE ITS REPORT CARD DAY." He screamed.

He squared up with Ledarius. "I got the same sixth sense as Common. Yeah, that's right, I can see the bitch in you, Ledarius!" He taunted. "Yeah, I bet yo' momma even know you a bitch. You don't think a mother knows when her son is a bitch?" his taunt grew louder. "I bet the day you was born, and your mother first held you in her arms she took one look at you and said to herself, 'Look at this little bitch.'" Ledarius jumped into his fighting stance, which was exactly what Damn Straight wanted.

"Yeah, come on," Damn Straight said, jumping into his fighting stance, he was geeked that he had finally provoked Ledarius into fighting him. Then they heard a banging sound on the door; it was Master Yang.

Dajon went to find him. "Master Yang, sir, I left my book bag in the locker room, but I can't get the door opened. I think it might be stuck. Can you help me?" They went to the locker room, and Master Yang tried to open it. It wouldn't budge so he banged on the door and yelled for whoever was in there to open it.

Dajon ran in and said, "There y'all go. I was looking all over for y'all. See, Master Yang, Ledarius said I should learn the crane technique first, but then AK wanted to teach me the deadly tiger style, so we was trying to figure out which one to start with first."

"Well, Dajon, you are most fortunate to have two very skilled young men offer to train you. Very good," he said.

"Yeah, and after this, we gon all go take pictures." Dajon said and then he and Ledarius got their things and left the locker room. AK was pissed, but he played it off and quietly vowed that Ledarius was going to get that ass whooping if it was the last thing he ever did.

18.

Brothers

"If I could swap your karate ass out for a brother that's a rapper..." - DeQuan

Quan was on the front porch of his grandmother's house when a car pulled up in front of the house and parked. "What up, CK?" Quan said as he stood up and walked down the steps to meet his friend. CK and Quan had forged a friendship despite being from different neighborhoods. CK had made a bunch of money in the streets and was starting to use it to fund his rap career. He pulled up bumping a song called "Beat Dat Body" by a new up and coming rapper from his neighborhood.

"What up, G-Quan?" CK said as he walked up to the porch. "Yo, what up with you, cuz?" Quan said as they shook hands. "Trying to smoke good. I was in yo' neck of the woods, so I had to stop by and holla at my boy," he said.

"Yo', this nigga right here crazy," CK said to his boy, who had jumped out of the car and came on the porch with him. "Remember that time you knocked that goofy ass nigga out that tried to rob us by Lemelle's?" Quan asked CK and smiled as he recalled the memory.

"Hell yeah." CK replied.

"I was just telling some of the guys about that shit the other day, how you snatched the blick out of old boy hands that time," CK explained, and they both began to laugh.

They both recounted the story of how they went into Lamelle's Sports Bar on 87th Street to go holler about some business, and as they was leaving, a dude tried to walk up on Quan and up that thang on em, and told Quan and CK to get on the ground.

Quan, having had a brother like Ledarius, had learned a few things of his own from him over the years. The one thing he wanted to learn the most was how to disarm someone if they ever pulled a gun on him at close range. So, when dude pulled the pistol on Quan, Quan did a quick move and snatched the gun from him so fast, that Quan, now had the boys pistol pointed back at him. Then CK immediately stole on him— Bam! —and hit the dude in the face, dude hit the ground and they both stood over him and punched him in the face a over and over.

Quan kneeled next to the would-be robber and put the pistol up to his head. "Man, I should put two in yo shit" He spat and then he went through the dude pockets and took everything out and found his ID and read his name out loud. Then he put the ID in his pocket and kicked him in his ribs. "Boy you better not ever come around here again, and I'm keeping your shit too, nigga." He added, and as they walked away, CK kicked him in his stomach again for good measure before they left.

They sat around smoking and trading war stories for a while, and then Quan asked CK to keep his ear to the streets, because Kaos was missing in action, and that was a headache he didn't exactly have enough Tylenol for.

Later on that day, when Quan got home, he went into the bedroom to put his money into the shoe box when he found Ledarius in the room trying clothes on.

"Quan, are you ashamed of me?" Ledarius asked while looking in the mirror and turned to go sit down on the bed across from his brother.

"What?" Quan replied as he locked the door and reached underneath the bed for his shoebox.

"Ashamed of me, like they way Richie was ashamed of Leroy?" Ledarius asked.

"Hell nah, man. Why would you ask me something like that?" he said, counting out his money on the bed in stacks of ones, fives, tens, and twenties. "I mean, you a little lame sometimes, but, you my blood, I would never be like, 'Oh don't tell nobody you my brother' or no stuff like that, 'cause at the end of the day, pssst," Quan made a sound with his mouth "We all we got." l talk my shit, cause that's what I do." As he continued counting silently to himself. "Now, where is all this type of talk coming from, Dare?" he asked, looking up for the first time.

"Nowhere, never mind," Ledarius said as he stood up and gathered up some things to take up to the roof. "Now, if I could swap your Karate ass out for a brother that's a famous rapper, you'd be gone before you can say 'Wax on, wax off.'" Quan laughed, completely amused with himself. Ledarius smiled and headed up to the roof as Quan sat in the bed, organizing his money.

19.

First Date

"Well, you walk around by yourself and read books and quote all these philosophers" - Brooklyn

Brooklyn was woken up by Cali, who must've been having a bad dream because she was talking in her sleep and tossing and turning. Brooklyn was nervous about waking Cali up at first, but after watching her for a few seconds, she gently put her hand on Cali's shoulder and shook her. "Cali you, okay?" she asked almost in a whisper. "You can't burn angels on the fire," Cali said in words that were almost indistinguishable, but Brooklyn heard her. "What?" Brooklyn asked, trying to see if Cali knew what she was talking about. "What?" Cali said, sitting up and rubbing her eyes. "Never mind," Brooklyn said, lying back down even though she knew she wouldn't get back to sleep.

They eventually both got up and went to the Rec with everybody expecting more drama, but there wasn't any because AK didn't show up. Brooklyn told Ledarius to wait for her after class and don't leave until she was done. When Brooklyn came out of the Rec later that day with her book bag, she told Ledarius that she was leaving and that if he wanted to join her, then he was more than welcome

They went and grabbed food, and then went back to the Rec to eat. "What's the deal with you, Ledarius?" Brooklyn asked while she dipped her French fries in her ranch dressing on the side.

"What do you mean?" Ledarius asked. "Well, you walk around by yourself and read books and quote all these philosophers and stuff," she said with curious eyes. "Reading is imperative for anyone who is seeking knowledge," he responded.

"Yeah, but the guys give you shit because you gotta admit you do *act a bit different*; shall we say?" She picked up another French fry and dipped it in the ranch. "How am I supposed to act?" he asked with genuine interest. "No, I mean you gotta be more street, you know? So, nobody messes with you," she said playfully.

"I am not really worried about anyone messing with me," Ledarius said. "I don't see why I have to act like everyone else. I am only being myself," he said, trying to understand why people thought the way that they do.

"Besides, what I see in the streets is death and incarceration, and those are not the paths that I choose to take," he told her, and for the first time, he made her realize that being street may not necessarily be the best way to survive at all. "Well, I never really thought about it like that," she said and finally let go of her expectations of what she thought she wanted Ledarius to be.

"Well, what do you like to do—I mean, besides Kung fu?" Brooklyn asked, trying to find a new compromise in their conversation.

"I like to read and exercise. Sometimes, my brother and I play video games," Ledarius replied, realizing that maybe he was a little boring.

"Well then, what's the last book you read?" Brooklyn wanted to know, really becoming interested. "A book by Niccolo Machiavelli called *The Mandrake*," he explained.

"You mean like Drake, the rapper?" Brooklyn asked, sounding a bit confused.

"Who?" Ledarius asked her.

"You don't know who Drake is?" she asked, sincerely surprised.

"I don't listen to very much rap music," Ledarius responded, feeling a bit embarrassed. "Wow, I gotta put you on, man," Brooklyn said with a smile. She pulled out her headphones and handed them to Ledarius, and then she pulled out her phone so that she could find the perfect song to introduce someone new to Drake's music. She chose, *"KiKi, do you love me? Are you riding? Say you'll never ever leave from beside me."* Ledarius listened for a second and started bopping his head to the beat.

They finished eating, then they got up and left, they went and walked and talked and made googly eyes at each other. They became more comfortable with each other, especially Ledarius, who finally felt at ease in her presence. All the talk of martial arts and books made Brooklyn think to herself that Ledarius and AK actually had more in common than they thought.

Even though he wasn't like the type of guys that usually tried to talk to her, the more she got to know him, the more she actually got an understanding of his silent strength. And she not only felt safe with him, but she liked the fact that he wasn't like everybody else, and she loved the fact, that she felt like she had a boy that was all to herself.

Ledarius walked Brooklyn back to where her mother was coming to pick her up. They sat on the bench in front of the center and made more googly eyes at each other until Nikki pulled up. Brooklyn wanted to kiss Ledarius, but she decided the time wasn't right. Plus, she needed to make him wait a little longer; she didn't want him to think she was a hoe. When Nikki finally pulled up, Brooklyn played it cool and gave Ledarius a hug. She was surprised by how strong his arms were, and he was blown away by how soft she was and how wonderful she smelled. She got up still holding his hand until she realized and gently released it. A few seconds later, she smiled again and headed towards her ride. Ledarius followed her with his eyes. He was on cloud 9 and didn't want to come down. When she got to the truck, she turned around one last time and made eye contact with him, then she jumped in the front seat with her mother and waved goodbye, and they pulled off. He could feel his heart follow her. He got up from the bench and headed to the bus stop, occasionally looking around to make sure that AK wasn't about to jump out of the bushes and suddenly attack him with his new diabolical alter ego.

20.

First Move

"Naw bruh, I don't give a fuck about that" - Maine

The next day, Brooklyn and the girls were in dance class when one of Dajon's protégés, Bug, ran in and yelled out that somebody was about to fight in the back. The girls looked startled at each other and then everybody ran outside. When they got out there, Maine was in Ledarius's face, trying to provoke him. It was on, and the kids knew what was about to go down and some of them began pulling out their phones.

Maine swung at Ledarius, but Ledarius easily avoided the punch. Then he swung a few more times, with Ledarius dodging each one, not really wanting to fight him back. Ledarius tried to plead with Maine that he didn't want to fight him, but it was too late, the plan was already in effect.

"Nah bruh, I don't give a fuck about all that!" Maine shouted, and then he went after Ledarius again.

"Come on Ledarius." Dajon, who was wearing the green Boston Celtics Rajon Rondo Jersey, whispered to himself while holding up his phone recording the whole thing.

Maine began to get mad and rushed in, but Ledarius easily blocked everything he threw. "Break 'em Maniac, send 'em out of here on his back!" Psyke shouted, but Maine couldn't seem to land a punch on Ledarius, and now he was starting to get frustrated.

Brooklyn looked nervous, and then she started yelling at AK. "Oh, so you gon' send your boy to fight your battle for you?" Then she ran over to try and break it up, but Psyke grabbed her. "Let me go," Brooklyn shouted as she struggled to free herself. When Ledarius heard her cries, he looked over for a split second, and Maine got the drop on him and kicked him dead in the chest, hard, *BOOM!* and sent him flying backwards. Everybody was like "Daamn!" Ledarius hit the ground, stunned and then he pulled himself up and when he got to his feet, something inside of him clicked.

Maine rushed him again, but this time Ledarius was ready for him, he unleashed a barrage of super quick punches that Maine wasn't ready for and kicked him right back in his chest and sent him flying to the ground. The ferocious look in Ledarius's eyes caught everybody off guard. The calm, shy boy they thought they knew was nowhere to be seen and what they were now witnessing was someone a lot more dangerous.

Maine was in trouble, and he knew it. He got up and charged towards Ledarius. Ledarius unleashed another vicious combination of punches and ended the assault with three brutal elbow strikes, then he grabbed him by his wrist, wrapped him up, flipped him over, and slammed Maine hard to the concrete. "Oh shit," somebody shouted.

It was becoming obvious now to everyone that Maine was outmatched, and then Brooklyn barked, "Let me go," and pulled away from Psyke, who was still restraining her. The second she broke his grasp and moved out of the way, Ledarius flew in with a knee strike right into Psyke's chest knocking the wind out of him and sent him to the ground hard.

Psyke got back to his feet, and Ledarius was all over him with lightning quick punches until he completely overcame Psyke's defenses. Everyone watching was in shock at what they were seeing with a selective few who were loving every minute of it, except for AK, who was watching from the side with Tick and Fang on each side of him. Maine rushed in to help Psyke, and Ledarius continued his brutal assault on both of them. He flung Maine into Psyke and broke both of them down. He hit Psyke in his throat, and he went down again and caught Maine with a hard punch to the face and it was lights out. Blood splattered everywhere, and AK had decided that he had seen enough, so he, Tick, and Fang decided to discretely remove themselves from the scene.

Psycho and Maniac were both on the ground bleeding and defeated, their plan to World Star Ledarius had backfired on them. When Brooklyn looked around for Ledarius, he had vanished, but Dajon knew how to track him down and had caught up to him and offered his services to be his manager.

"Yo', that was bomb as fuck. I'm about to post this right now," Dajon bragged as he fiddled around with his phone.

"No," Ledarius objected. "I'm on probation. I am not supposed to be fighting," he responded nervously. "Aw damn, that's right. Well, whether I post it or not, with all the kids that were there watching, man, they probably done already posted it, to keep it a dollar with you," he told Ledarius, knowing it was the last thing he wanted to hear.

Ledarius was worried about his probation officer seeing a video of him fighting and revoking his probation and sending him directly back to jail without passing go, or collecting two hundred dollars, Dajon, on the other hand, was trying to see how he could capitalize off the situation.

"Yo', you need to let me be your manager. See, we need to get some t-shirts made. We need to be thinking about merchandising and branding, monetization, Ledarius... monetization." Then he started doing some kind of dance he called his "Monetization Dance." He was moving his legs from side to side and flailing his arms around, doing his little dance, while Ledarius tried to figure out how not to go to jail.

"Come on let's go" Ledarius said and started heading towards the bus stop with Dajon behind him talking about trademarking his name.

21.

Moochie

"Do you know who David Copperfield is...? " - Moochie

Quan was sitting on his grandma's front porch when a blue, 1983 Box Chevy on chrome rims pulled up, and then a muscular arm came out of the driver's side window and signaled for him to jump in. Sitting in the back seat was Moochie. Moochie had a few problems he wanted Quan to solve with the utmost urgency. Since Quan introduced Moochie to Kaos and Kaos stole from Moochie, he held Quan responsible, and Moochie was not the type of guy you wanted to be indebted to.

"You know why I'm here?" Moochie asked Quan in his deep baritone voice.

"Because you were in the neighborhood and decided to drop by?" Quan responded.

"Oh, that's funny. You a clever muthafucka!" Moochie said. "No, 'cause I have a problem, and that problem is eating away at my tranquility DeQuan," Moochie explained.

"I'm sorry to hear that," Quan replied. "Oh yeah, you little smart mouth muthafucka? Well, I'm sorry to have to inform you that your friend Kaos—you know, the one you vouched for—has suddenly pulled a David Copperfield. Do you know who David Copperfield is DeQuan?" he asked with genuine politeness in his voice but with a seriously dangerous undertone. "He a magician," Quan replied.

"You damn right; he a magician," Moochie replied, dumping the ashes of a cigar out of the window.

"You know what his MO was? That muthafucka knew how to disappear. But you know what? I'm a magician too, DeQuan. I'll make a muthafucka disappear real quick, like that," Moochie said, snapping his fingers for emphasis. "Now, what I need for you to do is find that sticky finger little muthafucka and either bring me back what he took from me, or bring me back his head in a duffle bag, DeQuan. Or his debt is going to be transferred into your account. Now I suggest you make that your number one priority, DeQuan." Moochie explained to Quan with a look in his eyes and a tone in his voice that let Quan know that he meant business. Quan had already seen Moochie kill people that he had appeared to care about just minutes before he pulled the trigger.

Quan got out of the car as Moochie and Bruza pulled off. He stood there for a second and checked his phone. Then he walked back to the porch where Stimey was standing at the top of the stairs. Stimey didn't say anything; he just sat the grey book bag down, in the corner of the porch and took a seat and started rolling up. Stimey and Quan had something like a telepathic connection with each other, where they understood things without needing to speak actual words.

They sat on the porch and smoked in silence while Quan tried to figure out what was going on and what his next move was. Stimey wasn't much of a talker anyway; he'd rather watch, look, and observe. He had in his blood that "gangsters move in silence" type of mentality.

Once, he and Quan were at a party with a couple of other guys who worked for Moochie, and were peeping at some guys hating on them and plotting to set them all up. Stimey didn't say anything to alert the guys; he just started shooting. After they got out of there and made it back to their side of town, they asked him what happened, and he told them what he saw taking place. When they asked him how come he didn't say something to them, he simply responded, "I don't know." They thought he was crazy, but Quan understood, and to Stimey, that all that mattered.

They started making calls and trying to figure out how to get in touch with Kaos before Moochie made his way back around the block. It was better to hit him up before he hit you up. Quan wondered how far Moochie was really willing to take this whole thing. He hit up a couple of the guys to get a ride to come scoop him and Stimey, so they could bend a few corners.

22.

The Views

"I put that Serena Williams on that bitch" - Cali

"Yo', it's at 847 views." Jacob said, looking at his phone and referring to the video of the fight. He, Psyke, Maine, Cali, Brooklyn, and the rest of the girls were in a restaurant ordering food. Camisha and Teneshia sometimes messed around with Maine and Psyke. Jacob, Cali, and Brooklyn were just along for the ride.

Some guys in all black walked in and stood behind them. "Damn," one of them said, looking at Psyke and Maine, who were badly bruised up from their fight earlier. "We was just about to rob y'all! But shit, y'all look like y'all den already had a rough day," they said.

"Really nigga?" Cali said.

"Well, thank you for not robbing us!" Teneshia said sarcastically.

"No problem," the tall one with the dreads replied as he turned around to the other one. "Well, since we in here, you wanna grab a bite?" he asked as if just a second ago he didn't come in there to commit a violent felony.

"Yeah, I could eat," his friend replied nonchalantly.

"Really?" Cali said. "I guess robbing muthafuckas all day can really make a nigga work up an appetite huh?"

"Man, like you wouldn't believe," one of the would-be robbers replied. "And for your information, we don't rob muthafuckas all day," he added as if he was genuinely offended by her comment. "Just sometimes," he clarified.

"Ohhh," Cali responded as she rolled her eyes. "Well, how about the next time you wanna rob somebody, why don't you just rob a McDonald's instead, and steal you a couple of applications?" she said sarcastically.

"Why would we have to rob it? I'm sure they would give us a couple of apps if we just asked," one of them said as if Cali was the one sounding ridiculous.

"I'm so through with y'all," she replied, turning her attention back to her friends.

Brooklyn was looking at somebody she thought was one of the girls they went to grammar school with, who had jumped her and Cali in the bathroom back in the day. "Look, that's Marlesha from Foster Park sitting over there. Don't look," Brooklyn said to Cali, which prompted Cali to immediately turn around and look.

"Nah, that ain't her," Cali responded.

"Yes, that is with your blind ass. That is her, look, and she pregnant," Brooklyn replied. "What you doing?" Cali asked Brooklyn who was getting up. "I'm 'bout to go over and say hi," Brooklyn told her and walked over to the girls' table.

"Hey, girl," Brooklyn said in a totally different voice than the one she was just using a second ago. Marlesha looked startled for a second and then smiled. "Hey Brooklyn," she said and held her arms out for a hug.

"I put the Serena Williams on that bitch!" Cali boasted to Vanessa. "All you heard was *Whack! Whack! Whack! Whack!* The bitch was all discombobulated," and she made the motion of Marlesha being dazed and laughed.

"Hey, whatever happened to your friend you used to hang with?" Marlesha asked Brooklyn, who nonchalantly pointed over in Cali's direction, who was sitting there staring directly at them.

"Hey girl," Marlesha spoke softly as she waved at Cali, who was still sitting there looking, but did not acknowledge her at all. "She must not see me," Marlesha said.

"Yeah, she must not see you," Brooklyn politely added. "Whats your Instagram?" Marlesha asked as she pulled out her phone.

After the shenanigans, Brooklyn walked back over to where Cali and everybody were sitting. "She said hi to you," she told Cali.

"Man, I ain't never about to phoney kick it with that bitch," Cali replied to the amusement of the rest of the girls. When they all got up and headed back to the Rec, Brooklyn saw Ledarius and told the girls she would catch up to them. She went and sat down on a bench beneath a tree and, like a moth to a flame, Ledarius walked up just as she expected he would.

Meanwhile, inside the Rec, Ms. Freeman had been speaking to different community organizers about a plan to put together some new after-school programs that would not only benefit the children, but also benefit the parents who could use the few extra hours to get home and relax before their kids got home from school, giving them a break.

Ms. Freeman had been a staple in the neighborhood for decades and really cared about the children that she looked after. She had grown tired of programs that did a lot of talking, but never really did anything significant to bring about actual results. She had been in meetings all day and was surprised to see her old friend Terrance X, who had joined the Nation of Islam when he was a teenager and credits them for helping him become a better man.

Ms. Freeman liked him because he was always immaculate in his suit and bow tie. He was tall and strong with broad shoulders and a genuine smile. He spoke with the patience of someone who was intelligent and God-fearing, but Ms. Freeman wasn't letting him off the hook either. She wanted real results when it came to these children out here dying in the streets, and she wasn't entertaining anything less. She wanted accountability.

"I think Brother Terrance, that you and the brothers should do more outreach to these children out here shooting one another. I think you all should at least make the effort. You know these boys are lacking leadership and guidance, and you know exactly what I'm talking about."

Ms. Freeman was referring to the shakedown in 1995 by the FEDS that saw a significant number of the gang leaders in Chicago arrested and jailed, which left the streets without the structure that had kept things organized for so long. That eventually led to a lot of the young boys on the streets to adopt more of the renegade mentality that was the precursor to the anarchy we now have today. "Now you know, I will go to war over these babies." Her vocal tone confirming that she meant what she said.

"Get some of them rappers that follow the minister to throw a concert and get everybody together and talk to them and tell them to put on boxing gloves or something, I don't know. But if you come up with any ideas, I'll be glad to listen. Now, if you can excuse me, I have a little fire to put out with some of my children here. But my door is always open." Ms. Freeman acknowledged and then she got up and walked him out to the front door, holding his arm and enjoying how strong he was and how good whatever he was wearing smelled on him.

"One thing about the Nation, Marcus, is that they do know how to build some fine men," Ms. Freeman said, walking back behind the counter to sit in her chair.

"Yeah, that should be their new slogan," Marcus wisecracked. "The people from C.U.B.S called and said that they would be here tomorrow between 1:00 and 2:00 pm," Marcus let her know while he was sitting at the desk face-timing his daughter.

C.U.B.S was a nonprofit organization that stood for Chicago United Brings Strength, and consisted of ex-gang members that have come together to give back to the communities that they were running around in when they were in the streets.

Ms. Freeman was getting ready for the big 4th of July event. The sponsors, guests, and caterers, as well as the DJ and performers, all had to be on point this year. She didn't want any mishaps with this show and made sure that she had all her bases covered for the big night.

23.

Smoove

"You sure look like a master to me"   -Brooklyn

"**H**ey, what's up with you? I heard that you were on probation and are here because it was court-ordered. Please explain." Brooklyn ordered Ledarius with an adorably stern look on her face. He was defenseless against Brooklyn; he knew it, and she knew it, so there was no reason for him to try to avoid telling her what she wanted to know.

"Well, a couple of years ago, my mother met a man named Smoove, and they began dating. Eventually, he started to stay at our house a lot. He drank and smoked weed in the house, and sometimes, they would argue and fight. Well, one night, my little brother and I were asleep and heard a loud crash that woke us both up. We sat up and listened to what was going on until we heard the sound of our mother being choked in the kitchen. We both jumped out of bed and ran into the kitchen. We saw Smoove holding our mother down on the floor. He was beating and slapping her. My little brother went crazy, and we attacked Smoove, punching him repeatedly with everything we could. Then he grabbed me and threw me into the kitchen cabinet, and my little brother ran to get his baseball bat while Smoove and I fought in the kitchen, once I was able to get him off my mother. He was drunk, so I was able to handle myself for the most part against him, being that he was still very much bigger than I was. I was able to fight him towards the front door, and then my little brother ran back out with the baseball bat, swinging like a madman and hitting everything. When we finally got him out of the house and into the hallway at the top of the staircase leading downstairs to the front door, I had saw him almost fall down the steps and I tried to catch him, but my brother came and kicked him down the steps and he fell and broke his neck.

He could have died, but luckily, he didn't. The police were already sitting outside of the bar on the corner, so when they were called, they showed right up. My little brother had just gotten out of juvenile hall, and if he had of gotten into any more trouble, it would have made things a lot worse for him, so I told the officers that I did it, and they took me to jail instead."

Brooklyn was shocked and a little turned on, though she hid it well. "Now I get it, and that's why you stopped going to Master Yang's?" she finally said.

"Yeah, after my mother and grandmother came up with the money to bail me out, I started working with one of Master's good friends every weekend in her garden to pay them back, and help my mother more around the house. It was at that time that my brother started hanging out and making money in the streets," Ledarius explained.

"Hey, if you want, my mom and I can give you a ride home this afternoon," she offered, hoping he would say yes. Ledarius didn't want to accept, but he wasn't ready to leave Brooklyn just yet, so he agreed.

Nicole pulled up in a Burgundy BMW truck, playing "I Like It Like That," by Cardi B and singing along. "Hey, Momma, can we drop my friend Ledarius off at home?" she asked, but told Ledarius to get in the backseat before Nicole could even answer.

"Where do you stay, Ledarius?" Nicole asked, looking back at him through her rearview mirror and then making a face at Brooklyn, signaling her approval. "On 87th Street right before you get to Honore," he replied.

"Ledarius is in the Kung Fu class Momma," Brooklyn told her, but she already knew that from the conversation they had before.

"Oh really? How long have you been taking Kung Fu Ledarius?" Nicole asked.

"About eight years ma'am," he replied.

"Oh wow, that's a long time. You must be a real Kung Fu master by now." Nicole said jokingly.

"I am no master." Ledarius responded.

"You sure look like a master to me." Brooklyn whispered under her breath, twirling her fingers through her hair.

"You say something Brook?" Nicole asked.

"No, Mama," she shot back quickly.

"What do your parents do Ledarius?" she asked.

"Well, it's just my mom and little brother, but she works at the Marriot downtown. She is a front desk agent," he responded.

"Oh, that's a beautiful hotel. We had a seminar there once and I loved it," she said. "And what grade are you in?"

"I'll be going to my junior year," he replied.

"Ok, what kinda grades do you get?" she sharply added.

"Mom, what's up with all the twenty questions?" Brooklyn interjected.

"All A's ma'am," Ledarius replied. "All A's, no B's?" she asked.

"I got a B in my freshman year because my US history teacher didn't like to be challenged in front of the other students, so he became overly critical." Ledarius explained.

"Well Ledarius, you seem like a very nice boy, and I'd love to have you over for dinner sometime," Nikki said, knowing that inviting Ledarius over would make Brooklyn cringe.

"I'd like that, and thank you for the ride," Ledarius replied as they turned onto the side of his building so he could get out.

"Bye Ledarius. I'll see you tomorrow," Brooklyn said, turning around with a bright smile and a sparkle in her eyes that made Ledarius melt every time he saw them. He got out and headed up to the front door, eagerly looking forward to seeing her again tomorrow. Nikki and Brooklyn waited until he went inside before they pulled off eagerly awaiting their chance to start discussing all the Tea.

24.

Fang

"You gotta be smart out here, cause being stupid can get you killed" - Marcus

"Yo', you got 14,348 views on this video man. You a star now Jet Li Darius. We gotta start thinking about the big picture, appearances, and all the perks that I'll be partaking in." Dajon, who was sporting the Kentucky Wildcats Rajon Rondo College Jersey, explained to Ledarius as they walked down the hall. Then, two cute girls walked by in the opposite direction, and when they saw Ledarius, they smiled and made googly eyes.

"You see that? They love me!" Dajon blurted out. "I don't know what it is about the kid that drives the ladies crazy like that. I couldn't tell you if I tried. Maybe it's the mustache coming in." He rubbed his bald top lip. "Or maybe they like this smooth, hairless, prepubescent body," he said, rubbing on himself.

"No, I don't think that's it at all. Actually, I think you might be a little bit confused," Ledarius said.

"Well, I think you just might be a little bit of a hater," Dajon shot back.

"I would never be a hater," Ledarius explained.

"Well, don't get mad when your girl wanna babysit me." Dajon continued his delusional fantasy. They went outside and sat down on the benches. Dajon started selling his candy to anybody who walked past as usual. "Come on girl, you know you want these honey buns. I got a delicious chocolatey Twix in here too. Don't act like you don't want one of these Kit Kats to take with you for later," he shouted at the girls walking past on his salesman swag.

Marcus came over on his break and sat with Ledarius and Dajon. "What's up Ledarius? What's up Dajon?" Marcus asked. "Hanging in there, like a loose tooth" Dajon replied. Marcus was a good dude, who genuinely cared about the kids that attend the Center. "What's up Marcus?" they both replied and gave him some dap.

"Master Yang said he would be in late again today, so you get the class going until he gets here," Marcus told Ledarius.

"Y'all staying outta trouble?" Marcus had a vape pen he would hit every so often. Now, he said that it was only tobacco in it, but sometimes it's been suspected that he might have had a little more than just tobacco in that thing, but no one knew for sure. "'Cause it's a target out here on the backs of young black males, and it ain't finna let up. We got poison in our food, poison in our water, and they even flying over our heads in planes spraying poison in our air. If we don't wake up and get some real money to protect our parents and our kids, we're doomed. These niggas are out here killing each other instead of the motherfuckas trying to kill them. Malcolm X looking down like, 'You niggas den really turned into some bitches.' The whole time, we got police killing us, judges selling us to the prison industrial complex, social media feeding our children false realities, the emasculation of the black male archetype, and the mainstream media spreading propaganda against us," Marcus stated and then he pulled out his phone to check his text messages.

"What propaganda? Niggas out here really is crazy," Dajon added with a chuckle.

"Y'all gotta be smart out here. Being stupid can get you killed," he told them when he finally looked up from his phone.

"Dajon, you got real potential to do something great in life. Don't get out here and graduate from candy to dope 'cause that will only get you two places. Well, you already know that. I forgot," he said to Dajon, who had briefly thought about his dad and uncle. "I didn't," Dajon replied. "But it's all good. It is what it is," he added and stood up to stretch his legs when the Mothership carrying AK and his crew pulled up and parked backwards in the parking space.

It was June 20th, and Tick was in the passenger's seat with AK driving and Fang and Psyke in the back seat when he found the song he was looking for, and screamed at the top of his lungs, "REST IN PEACE PRODIGY!" and played the classic "If These Walls Could Talk," by Mobb Deep. He was still grieving on the one-year anniversary of the day Albert Johnson, AKA Prodigy, had passed away the year before. Mobb

Deep was Tick's shit, all the B.O.A actually, but it was Tick who Prodigy's death affected the most.

The song had a Beethoven sample running over a Havoc beat, with the two flowing over it the way they always do. Marcus was done with his break and was getting ready to head back inside, so Dajon and Ledarius followed him.

Ledarius let the class know that Master Yang would be late and that he was instructed to teach the class in his absence. After about ten minutes of doing so, AK and the boys made an entrance, and immediately, the tension rose. You could feel AK had changed into his alter ego Damn Straight.

"Excuse me young lady," he said to Ledarius. "You need to go find a ballet class to teach so all of that estrogen pumping through your veins can be put to better use." Damn Straight stood in front of Ledarius as if he wanted to break his face in front of the whole class. He was breathing hard with the look of a crazed madman in his eyes.

"I'm gonna put you in some stripper heels and a little pink mini skirt and make you twerk for change, on the corner of 87th & Ashland." AK looked him up and down, waiting for him to do something. "And you better drop it low," Maine added with a threatening undertone.

"That's right Ledarius, you better drop it low." AK cosigned.

"I wanna see you bend over and touch your toes." Psyke randomly added. And then AK looked at him kinda crazy for a split second and said aggressively, "Psyke said you better bend over and touch your toes." AK repeated. "And wiggle with it," Fang added. "And Fang said you better wiggle with it," AK said in an even more overly aggressive tone.

Psyke and Maine stood behind him like they really wanted that revenge. Ledarius stood there unbothered and unmoved by AK's attempts to bait him into fighting. He looked at Ledarius with disgust. "Then, I'mma put you in a bright red wig and make you dance to "Poison," by Bell, Biv, Devoe, and you gon' sing all the words to it to, Jet Li Darius," he threatened.

"And you better get all the parts right," Fang chimed in.

"Even Micheal Bivins part," Tick added. Then AK got up real close to Ledarius's face, put his finger close up to where he was almost touching his nose, and said, "Especially Micheal Bivins part."

"Yeah, you seem like a real lipstick and eyeshadow type of guy to me Ledarius," AK said, not so much like an insult but like he was concerned about him. "And you posing around here like a real martial artist, and that makes me mad." AK said, slowly ratcheting up his aggression again and flexing his muscles.

"Nah, that ain't why you mad. Go ahead and tell everybody why you really mad unless you're scared," Ledarius said, standing up to AK for the first time.

"SCARED?" AK roared. "SCARED?" He roared again with a wicked look on his face. "Nigga, I'll call Charlemagne right now, and tell him to put Angela Yee on the phone so I can tell her how cute she looks, and then, I'll have her put DJ Envy on the phone, so I can…TELL EM WHY I'M MAD!, to the whole ghat damn world, Ledarius, before I ever be scared of you." AK shouted and flexed his muscles again with his fist balled.

"I am not going to fight in whatever twisted game it is that you're playing." Ledarius shouted back.

"Who told you you had a choice? Fang, break him," he screamed, and Fang jumped out and went after Ledarius. Fang was bigger and stronger with a well-sharpened killer instinct, which was something Ledarius didn't have.

Ledarius was able to defend himself and block most of what was thrown at him, but Fang was strong and determined. He hit Ledarius with some hard shots and threw a punch that could have broken his jaw if it had connected. Then Fang threw an elbow strike that Ledarius defended and then let loose his own flurry strikes that caught Fang off guard. Ledarius had his own period where he studied Muay Thai briefly, and by studying, I mean he watched the tutorials on the Ong Bak DVD for about two months straight and practiced until he felt he could implement some Thai boxing into his repertoire. Well, now was his chance to test what he knew.

Ledarius caught Fang with some quick strikes. After finally getting Fang up off him, he hit him with some hard shots to the body, and wrapped him up, after delivering some damage of his own. He kicked Fang and then quickly closed the distance, then he hit him with a quick combination of fists and elbows, and after that, he caught Fang by the back of the neck and pulled him down into a deadly knee strike that hit with full force and knocked him completely unconscious.

Dajon's protégé Bug came in and yelled that Master Yang had just pulled up. Everybody began to scramble to get things back in order before he walked through the door. As they were dragging Fang out, AK looked at Ledarius. Now, it was all out war.

25.

The Hunt

"We got a runner, check every in-house, out-house, whorehouse and crack house" -Redrum

Quan and Stimey were riding around in the car with one of their boys, named Redrum, looking for Kaos. Redrum said he used to rap with Bump J before he got locked up, but that he couldn't take rapping seriously anyway because he was on the run for murder. They were bumping that Scarface "The Fix album." Chicago has always fucked with Scarface and The Geto Boyz since the beginning, and when the city found out about the man who put it all together, J Prince, who was the first person to do some things that the niggas in the city really respected, was a stand up guy, that built a connection between Chicago and Texas.

They pulled up on a block that had about twenty guys standing around outside. Quan pulled his gun out and cocked it, putting one in the chamber, then he and Stimey jumped out and walked over and shook hands with some of the guys. "Yo, y'all any of ya'll seen that bull Kaos?" he asked around, but no one had seen him. They hung out for a second and when they figured out, he was really in the wind, they jumped back in the car with Redrum and pulled off.

He drove all over, checking every place Kaos would be hanging, but nothing turned up. They finally went to JJ's to get something to eat. "Fuck, where dis nigga at, Joe?" Quan said.

"We gotta runner. Check every in-house, out house, whorehouse and crack house." Redrum said, laughing at his rendition of the speech made famous by the sheriff in the movie *The Fugitive.*

They bent a few more blocks, but no Kaos. In Chicago, you can't always just tell somebody where somebody else is like that, because you don't always know what's going to happen afterwards. You might tell somebody where somebody is, and then that person might end up dead, and then somehow you end up in it because you told him. Sometimes, it can be a real comfort to be able to say, "I ain't in it," because sometimes, being "in it" could cause you some stress or even some bodily harm or worse. So yeah, sometimes it's best not to know, especially with Quan and Stimey's reputation.

DeQuan and Stimey had a friend once named Lul Tee, who they had grown up with. He lived on 85th across from Foster Park and was killed when some niggas beef got heated and they went to handle it. He was an innocent by stander but was shot several times while sitting on the front porch with his little two-year-old sister. She survived, but Lul Tee died instantly.

The beef escalated with DeQuan and Stimey joining in on Lul Tee's behalf. That was what the city called a hot summer, with 762 murders being recorded that year. It was the summer of 2016 that saw a record number of homicides, and DeQuan and Stimey, and a few more of their friends were rumored to have been responsible for at least several of them.

DeQuan and Stimey were only 12-years-old when all of that took place, but the City of Chicago was no stranger to preteen killers. After that summer, everybody knew how Quan and Stimey got down, and most niggas decided that it wasn't worth the trouble. They even tried to blame them for the infamous incinerator murder, but nobody ever knew for sure.

They rode around for a little while longer, and then Quan told Redrum to take him to 87th and Marshfield. He spotted a Cadillac parked on the street, and then he told him to pull over and let him out. He got out, walked up on somebody's front porch, and rang the bell. "What up Unc?" Quan greeted him, shaking hands with an older gentleman who looked like he could be a pimp, maybe in his forties, who stepped outside and lit a square up. "What's going on wit'cha young blood?"

"Well, a bunch of shit. The nigga Kaos ran off on my plug, and now Moochie wants me to find the nigga and exact justice, but that boy ain't nowhere to be found." Quan expressed. "Y'all got it rough out here. It ain't like it was when me, Tim, Terrance, and Rob was out here," he said looking as if he was reminiscing. "That boy used to studder all the time, except for when he rapped tho. But, anyway, it ain't like it was when we was out here. So, how far you think yo man Moochie gone wanna take it?" he asked him, then he hit his cigarette and pulled out a diamond-crusted flask, which most definitely had some Hennessy in it, and took a squig.

"I don't know," Quan answered while giving the question some serious thought. Would Moochie actually kill Quan? It had never entered his mind before, but then it never had a reason to. "Well, young nigga, if you gotta ask yourself that question and ponder on the answer that muthafucking long, you might wanna start getting your affairs in order, if you know what I mean," he concluded.

"Alright Uncle Deno, let me get back in motion, Chuuch." He shook his hand. "Okay then, Chuuch. You be careful out here nephew," Uncle Deno replied and then Quan left and headed back to the car, jumped inside, and they pulled out. They ended up back on the block a little while later, empty-handed. Redrum dropped them off, and they went back on the front porch and rolled up. Quan had to strategize this out, before it got even more out of hand than it already was, and he needed a blunt to do that.

26.

The Room

"Don't lie hoe, you going to get chopped down by the lesser-known Power Ranger" - Cali

Brooklyn was in a hotel room, laying on top of the covers in her panties and bra. A half bottle of Merlot was on the nightstand beside her when the shower in the bathroom turned off, and the door opened in a cloud of steam. Ledarius emerged with water still glistening off his athletic frame. He walked over to the bed, looking down at the girl of his dreams. He climbed on top of her and began to kiss her gently on her shoulders and neck. His hands caressed her every curve, and his mouth followed right behind. He slowly kissed her all over her chest until he reached her willing nipples. He licked them gently at first, and after tasting her, he began to suck on them with increasing enthusiasm. He tongue kissed her softly while he rubbed her gently between her legs. He kissed her belly button, and then he slowly went down her stomach. He opened her legs and kissed her passionately through her panties. He licked her inner thighs, and then he moved her panties to the side, put his warm mouth directly on her, and began to passionately suck on her clit. He could feel her body respond, and he could hear the pleasure in her breathing. He somehow knew how to apply just the right amount of pressure with his tongue. He reached his hands up and grabbed her swollen nipples. Suddenly, the front door casually opened, and AK walked in. At first, he just stood there and watched them, and then he slowly pulled his shirt off, revealing his muscular chest and tattoos. He pulled his pants off, walked over, and laid down next to Brooklyn. He grabbed her neck from behind and gently kissed her all over. The three of them passionately intertwined giving Brooklyn the most intense pleasure she had ever felt. Then, out of nowhere, the Atlanta-based rapper, and baby momma maker, Future walked in singing Rihanna's hit record, "Love & Affection." When he got to the chorus, Brooklyn snapped out of it and woke up. She grabbed her phone, completely annoyed by that ringtone at the moment and answered it. It was Cali.

"What you doing, B?" she asked almost suspiciously.

"Nothing, sleep. What's up?" Brooklyn responded almost guilty, knowing full well that there was no way that Cali could possibly know what she was just dreaming about. "Well, I'm going by Drastik's later to go over some beats and start putting together what we gon' do for the show at Mr. G's, so that way, you can at least have the beat to vibe to and start coming up with the routine while I'm coming up with the rap." Cali instructed.

"Okay, cool. Pick one I can get loose to." Brooklyn replied.

"Okay. I'm about to call Tick and the teenage dumb-ass nigga turtles to pull up and run me over there. I'll hit you later. What you about to do?" Cali managed to slip in.

"I don't know. I'll prolly just hang around today," Brooklyn said with her hands in her panties, pushing gently on her clit with her fingertips. "Don't lie hoe. You going to get Karate chopped by the lesser-known Brown Power Ranger, the one who shunned the spotlight." Cali laughed at her own joke, amused by her cleverness.

"HA HA!" Brooklyn fake laughed. "You just make sure you tell Tick to tell his brethren assassin or what the fuck ever to leave my boo alone, shit!" Brooklyn pleaded.

"Say no more. Call you later." Cali hung up, and Brooklyn just laid out on her bed and decided exactly what she was about to do for the rest of her day.

27.

The Visit

*"My brother should know better to speak on family business
to an outsider" - DeQuan*

Quan was in the kitchen making scrambled eggs for his "world-famous scrambled egg and cheese sandwiches," as he always liked to say. His chef's name was Chef Boy-Ar-Gee. His kitchen was full of smoke, but he liked it like that because he wanted all the smoke, and the fire alarm in the kitchen was sitting there just looking at him like, "I am about to go off." He was happy when he found some bologna slices still left in the pack in the back of the refrigerator to drop on that bitch.

Quan had half of a blunt of that kill in his Bob Marley ashtray, and he couldn't decide which one was making his mouth water more, the egg and cheese sandwiches or that half of blunt. Quan had a lot on his mind at the moment, but somehow, he managed to stay surprisingly upbeat. "You know, Ledarius," he sat down and bit into his bologna, egg and cheese sandwich, "if you want me to come up there one day to that Recreation Center and shoot that bitch up, just let me know."

"No, I don't want you to come up there and shoot up anything." Ledarius shot back, slightly bothered by how his brother so casually spoke about shooting up the Recreation Center. "Okay, but I'm just saying, if you did," Quan replied, slightly offended by his brother's tone. "Want me to come up there with the stick and empty the whole drum? Just let me know ahead of time, because sometimes my schedule gets a little hectic, and I might have to move some things around," Quan continued.

"No, I don't need you to come shoot anybody," Ledarius said, trying to let Quan finish so the conversation could finally be over. "Okay, but I'm just saying in case you change your mind tho," Quan replied, not understanding why Ledarius was sounding so annoyed.

Ledarius was on his way up to the roof to work out and meditate when his phone rang. "Hey, Ledarius you at home? 'Cause I'm on my way over," Brooklyn said from the other end of the phone, almost giving him a heart attack.

"Ahh yeah, I'm here. When are you coming?" he asked nervously.

"As soon as my Uber gets here in four minutes," she said.

"Okay, I'll see you when you get here." Ledarius said as his whole entire heart rate had suddenly changed.

Twenty minutes later, there was a knock at the door, and when Ledarius went to answer it, Quan jumped in his way. "Man, you can't just run to the door looking all thirsty, Hong Kong Goofy. Let me answer it, then you walk up cool like, dig? Do I gotta teach you everything?" Quan snapped.

"Who goes there?" Quan said, walking up to the door and taking his sweet time, then he finally opened it.

"Hey, is Ledarius here?" Brooklyn said in a soft tone.

"Hold on, let me see...Ledarius?" Quan yelled out as if he really didn't know.

He finally opened the door enough for Brooklyn to walk in. Her smile lit up the room when she saw Ledarius. He walked over and gave her a hug. He loved how soft she felt in his arms. Quan coughed. "Oh, this is my brother DeQuan," Ledarius said, catching on.

"Hey Quan, your brother told me so much about you," Brooklyn said politely.

"My brother should know better than to speak on the family business to an outsider," Quan responded and closed the front door behind her.

Ledarius invited her into the living room and asked her if she wanted anything to drink or eat, because he could fix her something really quick if she was hungry. Brooklyn said she would like something to drink, preferably some juice. Brooklyn looked around the living room and eventually made her way over to the bookshelf. She smiled at old pictures of Ledarius when he was a baby.

"Who are these girls?" Brooklyn asked, referring to the picture of four young girls sitting on a big rock that looked like it was taken at a beach somewhere back in the days.

"Well, this one is my Aunt Jasmine, and these are her friends. They were all students at the same martial arts school together in San Diego, a very long time ago. It was a rumor that one of her friend's, that one," he pointed to one of the girls on the picture, "had a younger sister that was kidnapped, and she and her friends went to look for her, and a lot of people ended up being killed." Ledarius explained.

"Massacred!" Quan shouted from the kitchen, repeating the long-fabled family story.

"A lotta people? How many exactly is a lot?" Brooklyn asked purely out of curiosity.

"A lot, allegedly." Ledarius replied.

"Forty-seven." Quan added as he sat at the kitchen table scrolling on his phone.

"Bullshit!" Brooklyn replied.

"So where are they now?" she asked, seeing how long Ledarius was willing to play along. "No one knows. My brother seems to think that they are contract killers or hit men or hit women I guess, or something like that somewhere. He has a really vivid imagination." Ledarius responded, wanting to change the subject, so he invited Brooklyn into the bedroom to get her away from Quan. Brooklyn looked at the picture of those four girls again and caught the eyes of the little blonde girl in the middle, then she turned around to follow Ledarius.

She walked into the bedroom, and the first thing she noticed was all the posters on the wall; Jet Li, The Last Dragon promo poster, Bruce Lee, Malcolm X, Tupac. She looked at poster of the Ruff Ryder's logo with DMX and the rest of them hanging over Quan's bed, and at the various trophies from martial arts competitions Ledarius had won and a football trophy DeQuan had won the one year he tried organized sports.

She sat on Ledarius' bed and continued to look around. Ledarius was nervous, and it showed, so Brooklyn, being the sweetheart that she was, decided to rescue him. "Why don't you come over and sit next to me?" Brooklyn suggested as she patted the space right next to her for him to come sit. Ledarius' heart was beating like Nick Cannon in Drumline. When Ledarius sat down, she stared at him for a while. She looked him in the eyes and then studied his neck, shoulders, chest, arms, and all the way down to his shoes.

She jumped up and turned on the radio. Then she pulled Ledarius off the bed. "C'mon Ledarius, and dance with me." She grabbed his hands and pulled him towards her. "I do not know how to dance," he said nervously.

"I'll teach you," Brooklyn insisted as she took her hands and moved his hips with hers.

They danced for a minute, and then she moved in slowly and kissed Ledarius on the lips. Then she pulled back and looked him in the eyes, and when she leaned back in, she kissed him again, this time adding a little more passion.

Ledarius was in absolute heaven. He felt things he had never felt before. Love songs he had heard on the radio began to make sense. He had one of those moments that every boy would remember for the rest of his life, and then Cynthia came home.

They came out of the room to Cynthia's surprise—she had never seen Ledarius with a girl before. She wanted to lay down the law about girls in the house, but decided that she would speak to Ledarius about that later in private.

"Oh, hey, you must be Brooklyn. I'm Cynthia, I am Ledarius's mother. I'm so glad to meet you. You are so pretty. Do you want something to eat, besides my firstborn?" Cynthia said, breaking the ice with a little humor. She was excited and relieved that Ledarius had finally brought a girl home.

"Momma, Ledarius tried to expose me to the birds and the bees." Quan chimed in because that was the best thing he could come up with to say.

"Shut up boy, and leave your brother alone," Cynthia said, shutting Quan down before he said anything else to mess with his brother.

Brooklyn hung out for a while and got acquainted with the family. She later called her mom to come and pick her up, and when she arrived, Ledarius walked her out and kissed her again before they got to where Nikki could see them. Brooklyn left, and Ledarius felt like he had ascended into heaven. After she pulled off in the truck with her mom, he went up to the roof. It was time for him to be ready for whatever AK had planned for him next.

28.

Condition Red

"That's what the required reading is for" - Psyke

"**B**rethren, I came up with the code name for the siege on the Coliseum," AK announced to the guys while they sat up playing Tekken 7 on the PS4, bumping music while they smoked weed and philosophized.

"Condition Red!" he said, almost going into his Damn Straight character. "Oh yeah, that shit hard." Tick smiled his approval and gave AK the brethren's secret handshake. "Condition Red? Where you come up with that?" Jacob, who was over there hanging out had asked.

"See," AK looked at Tick. "Niggas who don't complete their required reading be left out, looking lost and asking questions that they would already know the answer to if they simply completed the required reading," AK scolded Jacob. "That's what the required reading is for," Psyke added. "That's what the required reading is there for, you hear that?" AK repeated triumphantly.

"See, if you had read the required reading, you would know that Condition Red is the final solution in 'The Spook that Sat by the Door'

By Sam Greenlee, a book about a Black CIA agent that came to the city and taught a bunch of the street soldiers guerilla warfare and a bunch of other wonderful useful urban domestic terrorist tactics." AK explained taking full advantage of the teachable moment.

"Tick, what number is the spook on the required reading list?" AK asked Tick.

"Four," Tick replied.

"Number 4, right after Sun Tzu and right before the 33 Strategies of War," AK said as he hit the blunt and looked at Jacob with the utmost disgust, Jacob was not officially in the B.O.A, but he hung around in hopes that he would be one day, once he completed the required reading.

Tick's phone rang, and he pulled it out and saw that it was Cali. "What up, Cali Cosa Nostra?" Tick called her by one of her many rap aliases from over the years. "What up, Tickle Me Elmo?" Cali shot back. "Pull up on yo girl. I'm headed over to Drastik's to go over some new beats," she told him. She then hung up and threw her rap folder in her book bag, grabbed her favorite lucky ink pen, the one she wrote "Chicago vs the World" with last winter, and got ready to link up with her producer.

Cali was in a studio with a talented up-and-coming producer named Drastik, listening to a bunch of his beats for the show at Mr. G's. Drastik's family grew up two houses down from Ledarius and Quan's grandma. They had gone through about ten beats, most of them fire, but she was looking for *The One*. He said he had one he thought she'd fuck with and hit the blunt and then hit a couple of buttons.

Cali leaned back in the chair, hit her blunt, and blew the smoke out, vibing to the music again, trying to find her zone. Some guys knocked on the door and came in, talking loudly and pulling out more weed to roll up.

"Yo', what's up with yo girl Brooklyn?" One of them asked Cali as she sat in the chair, trying to recite some of her pre-written rhymes to the beat Drastik was playing.

"I ain't hooking my girl up with you so you can fuck her life up, you big dummy," Cali said, bobbing her head to the beat and holding the blunt in her hand. "What's wrong with me? I'm that nigga," he said in his own defense. "Exactly," she responded, ignoring him and turning her attention towards the mixing board.

Drastik found the beat he was looking for, and he was excited about it. You could tell because he made the face that producers make when they put on a beat that they know about to fuck you up. That boy Drastik hit that button and sat back in his chair real smooth like he was the Captain Kirk of making beats.

Cali was just about to tell him that and bust him out, but when the bass line came on, the melody instantly got everybody's attention. Cali bobbed her head, waiting in anticipation for the beat to drop.

When the drums finally kicked in, everyone started rocking. "That's it, right there!" Cali said with enthusiasm and re-lit up her piece of blunt that went out.

"Yo', did you hear about the Chicago's Got Talent showcase they having at Mr. G's on the 14th? Man, they gone have celebrity judges there like Chance, I think, and that girl Diamond from Crime Mobb," one of the dudes who came in earlier said, not knowing that they already knew about the show and that that was the reason they were there in the first place. Then they all started singing *Knuck if You Buck.*

"Throw that bitch on repeat," Cali told Drastik and stood up and started trying to come up with a chorus. One of the guys in the studio pulled out a bottle of exclusive Vodka and started pouring it into some red cups and talking loudly again.

"Aye, shut the fuck up!" Cali shouted, looking right at the dude that was just pouring his liquor and talking loudly. "What?" he snapped back defensively. "Shut the fuck up, that's what I said nigga, you need a translator?" Cali snapped. He looked at her, and she kept looking at him. The tension in the room had maxed out quickly, but Cali wasn't budging.

The dude felt some type of way about Cali checking him like that in front of everybody. He was disrespectful because it wasn't his session, and if you happen to be in somebody else's session, it's proper protocol to stay out of the way and definitely not disrupt anything, but he didn't give a fuck and decided to laugh it off.

"What the fuck you laughing at?" Cali yelled and turned her chair away from the mixing board and towards ole' boy. "Huh? What the fuck you laughing at" she shouted again sucking the air out of the room, and everybody got quiet.

The dude looked at Cali, and then he looked at Teneshia and Alikah, trying to assess the room. It's situations like this that be how shit pop off. "This shit look like a joke to you? You think I'm in this muthafucka joking, nigga?" Cali stood up out of her chair. The dude noticed Tick, Psyke, and Maine looking at him, and then he became more aware.

"That's the problem with you niggas. You muthafuckas out here thinking shit is a joke. Ain't nobody out here playing with you nigga. Get yo' smiley face ass up out of my session boy!" Cali screamed at the top of her lungs.

The dude took note of the three ninjas sitting quietly on the couch, and it wasn't at all a huge secret that Tick was more likely to shoot first before he'd ask you a question. The dude picked up his bottle, his pack of red cups, and the short of a Newport 100 he put in the ashtray to save for later. Then he tossed up the deuces and left just as fast as he had appeared.

Cali reached into her pocket, pulled out half of a zip of some gas, and threw it on the table. "Y'all can roll up whatever y'all want to out the sack. I'm 'bout to take this whole one to the face." Cali re-lit her blunt and turned her chair back around to the board. "Drastik, put the beat back on sir." Then she hit the blunt, laid back in the chair, and stared up at the ceiling fan, trying to catch that feeling.

The instrumental had thick 808's and a diabolical bass line, with some violins that layered the whole vibe perfectly. "Let me sit on it. Send it to my email." Cali stood up and hit the last of the blunt. She gave Drastik dap and told him she'd hit him up later, and then she, Tick, and the rest of the crew got up to leave.

Cali was known in the neighborhood because of her family. Her father and uncles were heavy in the streets, and her brothers were respected.

One morning, her father promised her that he would take her shopping as soon as he got back from making a run with her uncle. Her younger cousin was begging to ride with them, so Cali just left it alone.

Her cousin ran out of the house and went and jumped in the car while her dad was waiting for his brother to come out of the bathroom. He leaned down to Cali and gave her a hug, and then he put it on everything he loved, which he said included her, that as soon as he got back, they would go.

When his brother walked out of the bathroom, they left out the front door. As they walked down the stairs, some dudes were coming up the street and opened fire on them. They hit them multiple times and left them dead right there in front of their house while Cali's little cousin was in the backseat of the car that they were about to leave in, watching the whole thing.

Cali was devastated and still mourning the loss of her father and uncle, and then, not even two years later, she lost her brother in an accident. When he passed away, Cali discovered his little black 25. automatic hidden in a crate of records, and she kept it.

She was smart, tough, and talented. Cali had the sort of energy that people just gravitated to. She had a magnetic presence whenever she entered a room and a big spirit that always left an impression on whoever she met.

Cali had the beat she was looking for, and now she was headed home to come up with one of the biggest songs of her life to perform at one of the biggest shows she had ever done. She knew that it was going to be some major influencers in the building that night and she wasn't planning on doing anything less than fucking the city up.

29.

The Favor

*"The lust for money, when it takes precedent over morals
and integrity is the problem" - Sharif*

A K was driving around in one of the unmarked vehicles that didn't have the B.O.A insignia on it. It was a 1997, black on black Nissan Maxima he had modified and painted to look almost like his own version of the bat mobile. He pulled up across the street from a house that had a bunch of kids playing on the front porch next door. He parked the car, but he left the engine running. He sat in the car for a while and observed the block for a minute.

He was feeling a sense of accomplishment. He had finally created the budget from the cars that they delivered to Bones to cover the buy in fee at the Coliseum. The exclusive high stakes underground fighting tournament was the first phase of his master plan.

AK was one of the founding members of the Coliseum, but the age-old story of greed and jealousy that always seem to weave itself into every tale that involves the downfall of empires was no exception in this case. AK was cheated out of some percentages that not only did he work for but were actually ideas that he came up with in the first place. The fight that he was preparing for right now was both business and personal.

Which was why he was here at this house right now. He rolled up the windows and killed the engine. He got out and strolled across the street and walked up the steps and did a secret knock at the front door. An older gentleman answered the door, AK walked inside and took his shoes off.

"Come on in Andreas," the older gentleman who went by the name Sharif told AK and offered him a cup of Green Tea. He nicknamed him that because he said that if AK had his way the streets would look like a Grand Theft Auto video game. The house was fairly typical for a man in his fifties who read a lot and collected things. He had pictures on his wall of Nelson Mandela, Haile Selassie and Malcolm X. Sharif had traveled the world and collected pieces of art and books from all over the globe, he could talk for hours about subjects that were deep and controversial.

Brother Sharif was AK's spiritual advisor and one of his early inspirations for what would eventually become the Brotherhood of Assassins. He was an ex-gang member who emerged from prison with a more enlightened mindset and an aggressive militant outlook, he believed in only the advancement of melanated people, his followers had no political, religious or gang affiliation. They followed the doctrine of the Melanics Society, who believed they were the *Children of The Sun* and lived there lives according to certain principles that aligned with their collective philosophy.

AK always found himself in awe of all the Afrocentric artifacts that were all over the elder's home, not to mention the massive book collection of esoteric knowledge and wisdom he coveted so closely. He looked through some of the books on the shelf until he came upon a series called *The Secret Teachings of All Ages*. Then he found a poster size picture of Sharif and his brother Derrick standing in front of a red, black and green flag that looked to have been taking in the late 80's.

AK was there because he needed to borrow some things, but he knew that he would first have to listen to the old man go on and on about whatever lesson he was preparing to teach in the moment. AK was appreciative of the long history lessons, parables and philosophical teachings he had grown accustomed to over the years, even when he wasn't exactly in the mood.

AK was there for a particular sniper rifle among other things and quite possibly support if the situation at the Coliseum somehow got out of control. The Panamanians over there with Enoch definitely had guns and wasn't going to hesitate to use them. "Sit down, have a cup of Maca Green Tea with me." Sharif said as he grabbed two coffee mugs from the cabinet. "It has Sarsaparilla, Burdock Root, Turmeric, Collagen, Tongkat Ali and some peppermint leaves, I call it that Pow Wow." AK smiled at the old man's antics he had seen so many times before.

The old man sat in his chair and pulled his pipe out and filled it with something that wasn't weed exactly, then he sat his lighter down next to it and grabbed his tea pot. "You are having difficulties because you are too attached to worldly things, and you have become distracted by things that do not serve your purpose, so there is an internal conflict." He poured the tea in each cup and brought them to the table.

"The problem with a lot of black men right now is that most are living in false realities and cannot properly process their emotions. Fictitious images of themselves that they have constructed in their own minds have altered their self perception and when reality conflicts with that false image, then there is friction, that disrupts the vibration and then rage, anger and violence follow." AK thought about some of the dudes that he knew that he thought was pretty delusional and silently agreed.

"The lust for money, when it takes precedent over morals and integrity is the problem. When one gets caught up in the; *well, as long as you get the bag it doesn't matter what you did to get it*, philosophy, confusing it with survival, then that will certainly lead down a dark path, and once you cross that line over into the realm of evil, you in turn invite evil back over unto your side of the line." AK sipped his tea and gave the old man his attention.

"That fictitious self-image and the lust for money is not all, when you combine that with the inability to control your impulses then the devil's clutches are upon you. Now that leads us to the most important thing, which is the ability to control your emotions, that is the key to ascending to the next plain of consciousness, the root of all evil is not money, it is emotions. AK thought about what the old man said as he took another sip of his Pow Wow.

The old man picked up his pipe and grabbed his lighter and lit it, he inhaled slowly and blew out an enormous cloud of smoke. "Too many frivolous attachments and not enough integrity means you are dealing with your lower self, how do you expect to rise higher when you are a slave to your lower self?"

"Imagine with your mind that there is something of significant value to you, it could be money or whatever it is that is most precious to you. Now imagine that object of value has been stolen and the thief is escaping in a yellow taxicab, and you have to chase that taxicab on foot through downtown Chicago. If the cab is traveling down the street once it turns the first corner, you would lose sight of it."

"You would have to run as fast as you could to the corner before that cab turned the next corner and the next and the next because once you lost sight of the cab then it would be gone forever. And that is how the mind works of a person who can only conceive through the lenses of the lower self. Now picture chasing the same taxicab that held your most valuable possession, but instead of running on foot this time you have elevated above the cities buildings and skyscrapers like you would be if you were in a helicopter."

"You do not have to run to each corner constantly chasing the cab, because now you have an aerial view of this city, and you are looking down on the streets like a grid, now you can follow the cab every which way it turns, left or right it doesn't matter. You could swoop down whenever and retrieve what is yours. That is how the higher consciousness sees the world, through a higher lense, an aerial view if you will, and that Is the key to navigation through this crazy maze, and remember to keep your eye on the prize and never get distracted by what is going on down there."

AK was enlightened enough to picture what Sharif had just explained and got the concept completely.

He finally got around to the list of things he needed, which included the Sniper Rifle and Sharif took him to the room where he could get what he came for. While he was in the backroom, AK spotted something else that made his heart skip a beat. He stared with butterflies in his stomach the way a boy does when he sees the girl he loves. They were black and about the size of a mango. Sharif noticed his eyes, but AK thought he had read his mind. "Go ahead and take them but be careful, only you or Tick need to handle those." AK grabbed what he needed and a couple of the military hand grenades and put everything in a bag and threw it over his shoulder, then he grabbed the case for the sniper rifle and left.

"Here and take these to Cali for me." Sharif said as he handed him a small brown package that was tightly sealed. "I told her that I would send these to her when I got them in." AK accepted the package and gave Brother Sharif a quick hug and left, he walked down the steps and crossed the street, he loaded what he had just picked into the truck of his car, then he jumped in the driver's seat and peeled off.

30.

The Dilemma

"I'll take you to a fancy restaurant and let you order a la carte" - DeQuan

Moochie was making Quan nervous, so Quan made sure he had the blick on him everywhere he went. Quan knew the stories about Moochie torturing and killing people in the past that had been foolish enough to get on his bad side. Hell, the shit Quan seen the nigga do with his own eyes was enough to have him concerned. Now we're not going to say that Quan was scared, we are just going to say that he was concerned. He couldn't help but think that if Big Cash was here, he could've had all this squashed by now. Cash was one of the older heads that have known Quan and Ledarius since they were little and was a bigger boss in the neighborhood than Moochie was, but Cash is out of town, and nobody knew where.

Quan hustled less and made sure he always had someone watching his back. He heard Kaos had skipped town, so Quan decided to pay his baby momma's best friend Juju a visit. He had the guys find out where her momma stayed. Quan pulled up to the house and told Redrum to keep the car running. He opened the car door and got out, then he tucked the pistol in his pants.

He walked up to the front door and rang the doorbell, when her brother answered, he asked to speak to her. "Is Juju here?" Quan asked using his calm voice. "Nah, what you want her for?" her brother replied, trying to swell up like he was about to do something. Quan smiled and pulled the gun from his pants and grabbed the back of Juju's brother's neck real fast, then he put the barrel to his forehead, and then for some reason or another, he just sort of relaxed, like everything was okay now that the gun was firmly in place. Her brother's eyes were wide open now, with an intense look of fear and forgiveness in them.

"Baby, I just put your laundry in your bedroom on your bed, I already folded everything for you, all you have to do is put them up." His mom said from somewhere in the house completely unaware of what was taking place at her front door. "Yo', if your momma come over here, I'm a blow your noodle cup all over her clean clothes." DeQuan said in a voice that let her brother know that he wasn't playing.

"Now that we both on the same page, I'm here to find out if she knows where her slutty little friend at." Quan pushed the pistol into the spot right above his nose-bone and directly in between his eyes real hard so that it would hurt a little. "See that bull Kaos den ran off, like Forest fucking Gump, and I need to know where or I'm gone get real agitated, now you don't want me to get agitated do you?" Quan asked.

"Man, naw, she not here. I swear on my momma." the boy pleaded while Quan looked him in his eyes to see if he was lying or not. "Man, she came over here a couple weeks ago, and man Joe, I heard her tell my momma she finna take Kiera and move with some nigga that just inherited a house or something, and that they was about to move to, I think Memphis, I remember, yeah it was Memphis because it made me think of Young Dolph.

Quan, still holding the gun to Juju's brother's head decided to stick his head inside of their house and look around with the eyes of a hunter in the jungle, then he looked back at Juju's brother. "Man, I wasn't really gon' blow your brains out all over your momma's clean clothes." Quan said nonchalantly as if everything was all good now. "But you make sure you go up there and you put them clothes up like she told you to tho, okay?" Then Quan kind of slapped him on the face the way the Italians gangsters do in the movies and turned around and walked down the steps and jumped back in the car with Redrum.

After riding around with Redrum and being forced to listen to his mixtape all day Quan decided he was done, Redrum dropped him off at the house and Quan went and sat on the front porch. He usually had the crew with him, but now was one of the rare occasions where he was by himself. He rolled up, lit his blunt, and then he went into his phone and made a call to one of the guys he knew who had people down in Memphis, but it went to voicemail.

Quan hung up the phone and hit the blunt and blew the smoke out when a girl named Casey walked by the house. Casey was a skinny brown skinned girl with big eyes and a naturally curly afro who Quan had a thing for because she was different. He had never met a girl that was into biology and had dreams of becoming an actress. He walked down the steps and strolled up to her with a boiling pot of confidence.

"What's up Casey?" He said with a whole big Kool-Aid smile. "Why you be playing with my heart?" He said and licked his lips looking into her big doe eyes completely captivated by the cutest smile he had ever seen. "I ain't playing with you boy, what you talking about?" she replied flashing the smile that was currently melting his heart.

Down the street a black, SUV with '22-inch chrome rims pulled into a driveway a few houses down. "Baby, you the type of girl that'll make a real killa put the guns down, for real tho, I'm a take you to a fancy restaurant and let you order Al la Carte" Quan said trying out his version of ghetto charm and Casey laughed and flashed that smile again. "Hold that thought, as a matter of fact let me catch up with you later." Quan told her and headed down the street towards the black SUV.

He walked about four houses down and up the steps and knocked on the door. The door flung open and a large, tatted OG with long dreads named Huey answered. "Huey P" Quan gave him dap, walked in and sat down. Huey was older than Quan and Ledarius, but they had known him all their lives because he grew up on the block all his life just like they did.

"Yo', let me get a quarter," Huey said sitting back down on the couch, he had a rolling tray and a 45. on the table next to him. Quan pulled out a digital scale and put some weed from out of a bag he had in his pocket on it and weighed it out then he handed it to Huey and collected his money. Then he pulled out his personal sack and started to roll one up. "What do I owe the pleasure, Quan? I know you didn't come over here just to make sure my weed tray was full." Huey asked picking up the television remote to switch the channel.

"You heard about the dilemma I got on my hands by now, the boy Kaos is in the wind and Moochie got my top on the chopping block behind this shit, Joe." Huey was in the middle of licking his blunt so he couldn't answer just yet. "Yoo, I did hear something like that, then something hit me, one of the guys I did time within Joliet had some wild theory about your pops and his crew." Quan had the insight to quickly question in his mind before Huey got to it about whether or not he even wanted to hear what Huey had to say, but he entertained it, because curiosity really is a muthafucka.

"One of the niggas in there named Juice was bunkies with Moochie when he did that time in the county, and they was talking about the old days and your pops name came up, and Moochie having something to do with the robbery that got everything fucked up in the first place, and then he said something to the effect of, who would have the most to gain from your people being out the way?" Huey had a bottle of Hennessey that he almost offered to Quan before he remembered that Quan was only fourteen.

"This was after you, Stimey and The Rug Rats turnt up like ya'll did the other summer. I remember that was the whole reason for the conversation in the first place; something about you might become too dangerous one day if you ever found out, so it would be the smart move on Moochie part to get you up outta here before you got grown and started asking questions."

Quan had an epiphany, listening to Huey made some shit click and now he could spot all sorts of red flags. He stayed silent though and listened until he had the full story. "Why you just now telling me this G?" Quan finally asked Huey.

"I just thought about it, what? Your situation jogged my memory G, what you want me to say?" Huey said with the type of sincerity that made you just say forget it. Quan had heard enough anyway and needed to come up with the next course of action. He got up, shook hands with Huey and bounced out, then he called Stimey and told him to meet him on the porch.

31.

Post

"That's over a quarter of a million hits Ledarius" - DeQuan

Dajon for some reason was doing his monetization dance, which looked like a bootleg version of the crip walk, he was over by the benches where everybody hung out, with Brooklyn, Cali and the rest of the girls cheering him on. When Ledarius walked up Brooklyn was both worried and turned on by Ledarius after hearing about the fight with Fang. "You got 274,368 hits Ledarius." Dajon abruptly switched up and went into manager mode.

"Now this would be the part when I say, men lie, women lie but numbers don't, but don't get it twisted Ledarius, black folks always so quick to repeat what they hear another nigga say, numbers do lie Ledarius, they can be fabricated and manipulated, but these numbers right here, these numbers right here nigga." Dajon said going into his Katt Williams impersonation.

"But these numbers right here, I've done the math, and I trust the algorithm Ledarius, and these numbers say 274, 372. Oh, that's up four views since I even started talking," he stated with enthusiasm.

"That's over a quarter of a million hits Ledarius. You know what time it is now playboy? Monetize," he sang out loud and then he went into a full-on impromptu performance of his new hit single that he just made up on the spot called "Monetize Baby," soon to be available on all streaming platforms. Then he started singing.

"You gotta monetize, you gotta monetize, you better recognize, you better realize"

"You gotta monetize, you gotta monetize, you better strategize boy, you better organize"

Then he asked Ledarius if he wanted him to show him how to do the monetize dance that goes along with the record before it blows up, and then he started doing the monetize dance again.

"Don't be hating on me, cause I'm 'bout to be a star, and I'm 'bout to go to the Grammy's handing out fuck you's. I'm a be like fuck you! Fuck you! Fuck you! Fuck you! Oh, wait, I think I'm all out." He stopped and searched his pockets and then he checked his back pocket and pulled out an imaginary object and said, "Oh, I found one," he put his middle finger up and said, "fuck you," and everybody laughed.

"This Ain't What You Want," by Lil Bibby was blasting from somewhere in the distance, then the mothership pulled up. The sunlight caught the chrome on the rims, and they sparkled like diamonds, then they pulled into the parking lot and parked backwards in the space so that they could watch everything. Ledarius knew something was coming and got ready for it. Then Alikah looked at her phone and a few seconds later, showed her phone to Brooklyn. Then Cali looked at her phone and took a deep breath, then Camisha and Teneshia looked at their phones.

Then Dajon looked at his phone. "Let's go Ledarius, we got that thing we gotta do." Dajon said and urged Ledarius to follow him. They walked inside. "Hey Ledarius, come here for a minute." Marcus called from the front desk. Ms. Freeman had gone to pick out decorations for the 4th of July show.

"Hey, young brother." Marcus said in a low tone. "I been hearing bits and pieces about some things that's been going on around here, are you good? If you need me to get involved, you let me know, okay?" Ledarius appreciated the gesture but… "No, thank you" he said humbly.

"What is this thing we have to do?" Ledarius finally asked Dajon, once they had made it all the way to the storage area. Dajon turned around with his phone and handed it to Ledarius. "He's just trying to get in your head champ, messing with your mind, throwing you off your game." Ledarius looked in horror, his heart sank from his chest and sat heavy in his stomach, his throat was dry, and his eyes burned. It was a picture of AK and Brooklyn all hugged up on each other and cute, at what looked like somebody's house party. It was obviously from some time ago and the caption even had the hashtag #tbt, but it still hurt, and Ledarius was furious.

Ledarius went out of the back door of the Rec where the trash dumpster was and headed towards the bus stop. He had all sorts of nightmares going through his mind. The bus finally came and he jumped on it and it pulled off. He sat down on the back of the bus, and all his thoughts led back to that picture, and what details he didn't know, began to be filled in by his own imagination and that is never ever a good thing.

When he got home, he went straight up to the roof and began hitting the punching bag. The more he hit the bag the more imaginary pictures danced through his mind and the more ferocious the punches got. He stopped and he paced back and forth for a while then he went back at it again, furiously hitting the punching bag and feeling the full impact on his fist and in his wrist. Ledarius had been feeling plenty of things he never felt before for the past few weeks, but what he was feeling right now was trying to defeat him, and as of right now that feeling had the momentum.

32.

Coliseum

"Who' s Vic, My name isn't Vic, Do I look like a Victor to you" – The Uncle

A K and the brethren were at the house getting prepared. They were putting on all black clothing that looked like a cross between ninja suits and military tactical gear, but with a hood twist. All their clothing had the Red B.O.A insignia and were designed with trick pockets that concealed weapons and other useful tools.

Fang and AK were counting out the money they got the other night from the cars and were putting it into a black book bag. Tick was checking the black cases containing two AR 15's and the Sniper Rifle for the Shiite to have posted up outside the Coliseum as back up to make sure they had cover incase things got tricky. The Shiite was the oldest member of the B.O.A, and AK's ace in the hole. They gathered up everything just as AK had instructed and filed out of the house and into the Mothership.

They hit the freeway and rode about forty-five minutes out of town until they ended up at a warehouse in the middle of nowhere and pulled up to a huge metal gate. Tick gave the code and the security let them through. They drove in and parked, then a dark figure emerged from the shadows and AK popped the back. He opened the hatch and took the black case containing the sniper rifle and closed it back.

The boys got out of the truck shortly after and entered the building. They walked through several hallways and corridors until they entered the arena. The lights were bright, and the air smelled like blood and sweat. Tick walked in with AK, Fang, Psyke and Maine following behind him. Tick handled all the business, and he did all the talking. Tick took the duffel bag and walked up a flight of stairs with Fang, while Psyke and Maine slipped off behind a black curtain. AK searched the crowd like a wild animal hunting his prey.

Tick and Fang came back, and Tick gave AK the look, indicating that everything was a go. The fight that was taking place was between a white boy and a South American fighter. The South American fighter had a lot of fancy moves and lightning quick speed. He was working the white boy over with some quick combinations and serious knee strikes. AK was wondering where Psycho and Maniac were and just as he was about to send Fang to look, he saw Maine and he promptly gave AK the same signal as Tick.

The guy AK was looking for was in the upper level where those with the money and power sat. Enoch was Panamanian and black and built like a monster. He was bigger and taller than AK with a scar through his right eye, that left his pupil slightly discolored from the time a dude had robbed him and sliced him with a box cutter. The white boy fighting in the ring got a burst of energy and let his hands go, knocking the South American fighter to the ground and now had changed the momentum of the fight.

Enoch and AK had met on the red line a few years back and started talking, and that conversation somehow ended up with them discussing the movie *fight club*. Enoch was impressed that AK knew about the Author Chuck Palahniuk and had even suggested some of his other novels. Later they ended up forming a bootleg version of fight club and it grew and eventually turned into what the Coliseum is today. Once they started making money Enoch's Panamanian uncle wanted to invest and nobody was really in a position back then to say no, and eventually he took over.

AK and the brethren's obsession with assassins made AK maneuver with a strict logic and a precise emotional intelligence. He was not only able to leave with his brains still on the inside of his head but also an undisclosed amount of money in his bank account, but the business was now completely out of his hands. Tick wanted to go in and shoot the room up, but rule number 3 in the B.O.A Handbook states that you must think seven times before you act, so AK forever a loyalist to the doctrine accepted this as a teachable moment and charged it to the game for the greater good of the movement and moved on, but he never lost hope that one day he would circle back and reclaim what he built.

He plotted his revenge, and tonight was when phase one of his plan was set to begin. They sat in their section across from where Enoch and his people were and that kept the tension at a nice even temperature.

When the announcement came that there was a challenge, and the stakes was $100K the place went into a frenzy.

Enoch had no choice with a publicly announced challenge, and accepted just like AK knew that he would. He looked down at AK and then he turned and disappeared. The white boy caught the South American fighter with a sharp haymaker that did some damage and pounced on him. He overwhelmed the South American fighter and ended the fight in a dramatic upset to a loud uproar from the crowd.

Enoch, who also went by the name Knock, as in, he'll *knock* a nigga off, you don't want a *knock* at your door, or *knock* a nigga's bitch. He had a thousand ways that he would flip his name into a conversation. When he and AK started building what would become the coliseum. Enoch started doing collection work for his uncle and was using the guys from the fight club to get things handled.

Eventually greed kicked in and fucked everything up. Enoch wasn't exactly trying to do AK dirty; he just didn't have enough control over his uncle. Enoch knew better than anyone just how dangerous AK could be. Someone that crazy and ruthless with a brain like his was someone Enoch wasn't comfortable going to war with.

Tick and the rest of the boys kept their eyes on every section of the coliseum. AK was preparing for war. The fight announcer called their names, and they made their way to the center of the ring, and once the bell rang, AK and Enoch went at it over the course of the next three minutes. The crowd cheered and hollered, but it was those that knew what was really going on that was truly on the edge of their seats.

Even when the momentum seemed to switch between the two fighters, AK was never not in control and when the time came for him to end it. AK beat Enoch to the punch one too many times and landed a series of brutal combinations to finish him. Knock hit the ground, but his people jumped right in and kept him from going out bad. Enoch's uncle was fuming, but the boys was ready for whatever happened next.

AK had succeeded in making his statement and the boys moved into position to collect their winnings, but when they did, they were for some reason directed to the office upstairs. When they arrived, they were greeted by Enoch's Panamanian uncle and a room full of his goons. Enoch wasn't about to take that L he just suffered lightly and was ready to do something reckless. "Andre, let's discuss our options." Enoch's Panamanian uncle said trying to stall. "Giving me my money is the only option you got Vic." AK said with the confident swagger of someone that knew something that everyone else didn't. "Vic? My name isn't Vic. Do I look like a Victor to you?"

"Yeah, is that right?" Enoch stepped forward and put h hands on the gun in his waist band. When he did that, The BOA Boys all pulled their guns out at the same time just like in the movies and when they did that, all the Panamanians pulled their guns out too, also just like in the movies. It was what is referred to sometimes as a Mexican Standoff, with both sides ready to pull the trigger at any second.

"If we don't walk out of here, I guarantee you, that none of you will be able to walk out of here." AK said not even looking at Enoch, but at his uncle and then he stood in the center of the room being the only one without a gun. "That pistol don't make you tough bruh, and trust me when I tell you, your uncle knows that your reactive nature is a liability, and he also knows that I don't fear you one bit, gun or no gun." AK pulled something from his back. "Either way it go tho, it's gon' be some bloodshed." he added and revealed a live military hand grenade.

"Whoa, Aye what the fuck Dre? You are fucking crazy bro." Enoch yelled out and instructed his uncle to tell his guys to lower their guns. "Yo', yo', yo', okay, okay, okay, alright alright!" he held his hands up and called for everybody to calm down. "Give him his money." he told one of the guys who quickly left the room. "You got a lot of fucking balls, I'll tell you that kid." One of the older guys told AK. Enoch became instantly diplomatic and pulled AK to the side and told him that they would talk about making things right.

AK and the boys left the warehouse with a couple of the Panamanians who were making sure AK made it out safe and that there were not any snipers outside ready to pick them off when they left later that night. AK called off the Shiite, who was waiting outside in a nearby structure with the sniper rifle trained on anybody not in the Brotherhood, The Shiite had to give up his religion to gain entrance into the brotherhood. His loyalty was unquestionable which was why he was the insurance policy. When AK got off the phone, him and Tick looked at each other and laughed, and the rest of the boys settled in because it was a long drive back to the city.

33.

The Invader

"Hey, what you do to my brother?" - DeQuan

When Ledarius got home, he found Quan arriving home at the same time after having a long day of dealing with the drama currently taken place in his life. Quan wasn't much in the mood for conversation and Ledarius who had just found out about AK and Brooklyn's past didn't feel like chatting very much himself. When they walked in Cynthia looked at the both of them suspiciously. "Hey, what ya'll up to?" she asked half-jokingly and half serious. "Nothing" They replied at the same time sounding completely innocent.

"Well, I have someone I want you two to meet" Cynthia introduced him as Tony, and he got up from the living room couch and walked over and stood next to her. He was tall and good looking, with a body like he spent a lot of time in the gym. He was clean cut and handsome. "He works with me, and he goes to film school at Columbia. That's where Lena Waithe went to school."

"This is my son Ledarius," she put her arm around him and smiled. "And this is DeQuan my youngest." she said hoping Quan didn't say anything too crazy. "What's up little man?" he said to Quan who was completely offended by the whole little man comment. He gave him a fist bump and turned to Ledarius "What's up man? You look like you work out." Tony said and shook his hand. "To Ledarius and Quan, he looked like an infiltrator and an invader, but the Cynthia he looked like a whole meal.

"Well, I'm a get going, I got an early day tomorrow," he said, and Cynthia walked him over to the door and they gently hugged each other, and he gave the boys fist bumps and left. Cynthia turned around and smiled then she looked at the boys and frowned. "What ya'll looking at? Ya'll are not about to Jody momma me, okay? Momma got to have a life too." she said looking like she had time for the drama today.

Quan cleared his throat. "Okay, but for the sake of keeping everything copasetic, can you please inform him about what we did to the last one?" he said as if he was being helpful somehow. Ledarius who usually stayed pretty neutral in most situations when Quan got smart with his mother, chimed in this time and said, "As a deterrent," which led Quan to snap his finger and point at his mom and say, "Exactly."

"I'm about to close my eyes and count to ten, and when I open them which ever one of ya'll is still here, I'm punching you in the throat." Cynthia responded and the boys were smart enough to take the out and make their way to their room and let her have her peace, and plus both of them had issues of their own they needed to figure out.

Ledarius couldn't get the image of AK and Brooklyn out of his mind. The smiles on their faces and the sparkle in their eyes and the joyous expressions on their faces were ripping Ledarius apart like an aggressive virus attacking his heart and mind. Then in his head he heard the voice of Yoda, the little green Jedi Master from the Star Wars movies saying, that anger leads to hate and hate leads to whatever.

So, while Ledarius was contemplating whether he should turn to the Darkside of the force, Quan was thinking about killing Moochie if it had to come down to it. Quan had looked up to Moochie for as long as he could remember and had plans of world domination with his mentor Moochie by his side. He would be proud of what his Padawan had accomplished, like Obi Wan Kenobi and Quan was like a young Anakin, then he thought, oh wait, Anakin grows up, turns into Darth Vader, and kills Obi Wan. Instantly, that idea gave him a chill that he didn't like, so he dropped the thought from his mind and assured himself that something would work out and it wouldn't have to come to that and with that, he went to sleep.

The next morning the boys woke up and Cynthia, having to work an extra shift at the hotel had left them food to heat up in the microwave when they got hungry. Ledarius headed up to the roof to work off some steam and try to regain his focus. He hit the heavy bag until he was almost out of breath and then he heard his brother call out his name, "Dare." Quan shouted. When Ledarius turned around, he was shocked to see his brother standing there with Brooklyn and Cali.

Brooklyn was heading his way, and his heart was thumping at a million beats per minute. "What exactly is your problem, Ledarius?" she asked as she stumped over and stood in front of him with her hand on her hip. Ledarius was slightly thrown off by how beautiful she looked when she was mad, but he tried his hardest not to give in.

"So, you the muscle?" Quan asked Cali looking her up and down. "I'm She- Hulk in with a chip in my shoulder" Cali replied as she looked Quan up and down, He looked at her and shook his head, and decided to chill and see how things played out.

"Ledarius, that picture was taken before I even knew you." Brooklyn protested in her defense. "I did have a life before we met Ledarius." she pouted. Ledarius stood with his arms folded in front of him and Brooklyn grabbed his arm and delicately unfolded them. Meanwhile, Quan and Cali stood just a few yards away from them with their arms folded watching the scene in front of them like it was really Netflix.

"Ledarius" Brooklyn grabbed him and pulled him in and hugged him and when Ledarius attempted to pull away, she grabbed him between his legs and didn't let go. "Ledarius you really gon' let this keep us apart? You really gon' let me go over something that I don't have any control over?" Brooklyn refused to be derailed, she had come for her man and wasn't leaving until things were back to normal. Ledarius had all the blood in his body racing towards one region and Brooklyn could feel it beginning to grow right there in her hand.

Ledarius felt a wave of total bliss cover his whole body and then he panicked. He ran and sat down and covered his crotch with both hands. Brooklyn had worked her magic and was now looking at Ledarius squirm. "Hey, what you do to my brother?" Quan yelled out after seeing Ledarius fold. "Brooklyn walked over to Cali and gave her the look like the mission was complete. "Hey, I'm performing for the 4th at the Rec you should pull up." Brooklyn told Quan while he shook his head at his brother's defeat and turned to take the girls back downstairs and see them out.

34.

The Fourth

"Ok, you a good kid, I'm a trust you to keep things under control" -Marcus

It was the 4th of July, and the Rec was buzzing. It was more people there than any other night Ms. Freeman had ever seen before. The gym was decorated with colorful LED lights and streamers, they even had a Party City smoke machine blowing smoke into all of them poor kid's lungs. Marcus had hired a DJ who had brought huge concert speakers. They had black lights and glow in the dark paint and the kids was running around like the Lord of the flies.

The girls in the dance class were all dressed to impress. They all had their hair and nails done and some of the girls even had color coordinated costumes and make up. Brooklyn and the girls were sitting in the parking lot, in a car Vanessa had finessed from some older guy who let her borrow it for the night. Cali pulled out the bag she had got from AK earlier. "What's that?" Vanessa asked as she hit her little mini bottle of Pink Moscato and played songs from her phone on the Bluetooth.

"Just wait" Cali said pulling the tape off the package then she poured out the contents. "What's that? potpourri?" Teneshia asked pulling out her phone to use her flashlight. "No, but close, these my promiscuous young friend are rose petals." Cali held them in the palm of her hand. "And we are about to smoke these bitches." she said as she separated and crushed them up and sprinkled them on top of the weed and rolled them up in the blunt.

"It makes the high more euphoric and it has all kinds of medicinal benefits. Google it if you don't believe me." Cali insisted as she was just finishing up what she called pearling the blunt. Vanessa pulled out her phone and Googled "The benefits of smoking rose petals." She read it for a few seconds "Oh shit, listen, they have vitamin C and antioxidants, and is good for your skin. Damn, read all this shit!" she gave her phone to Camisha who began reading off even more benefits.

"How you find out about this?" Teneshia asked.

"Cuz I'm plugged with the information okay." Cali yelled and they sat in the car and smoked. When they were done, they went in the dance recital with their eyes all red and giggling, high as hell. They got up in there smelling like body spray and weed. Dajon was wearing a Rajon Rondo Sacramento Kings jersey with matching purple and black Jordan's. He had his protégé Bug with him and they were working the room like two professional swindlers with youthful smiles and a sugar rush.

Cali was in the DJ booth making sure he had everybody's music and testing the microphone so that he knew that she would be hosting tonight and that he should just get used to it. Alikah the African princess who wanted to go to school to be a film maker was overseeing production. She was into the creatives like Shonda Rhimes, Issa Rae and Courtney Kemp who are all out there trailblazing and pushing the boundaries, and hoped that one day she could be up there among them.

The twins were going over last-minute critiques with Brooklyn, and Vanessa was making sure the set decorations were just right. Dajon found Ledarius sitting off in the cut and went over to entertain himself and inform Ledarius of the current views of the last fight against Fang. Cali negotiated a truce between AK and Ledarius for the event because Brooklyn would lose her mind if her event got destroyed. AK accepted the truce on the basis that once it was over it would be open season on Ledarius and nothing short of an act of God was going to keep him from getting this ass whooping.

One of the sponsors for the event was C.U.B.S which stood for Chicago United Brings Strength. One of the speakers was a former gang leader who served over twenty years in prison, and since being released has started an organization designed to help give our youth and find other options besides selling drugs and gangbanging. AK and the boys walked in looking like the villains in a Batman movie, not the old school one but the Chris Nolan one with the much darker undertone.

Dajon looked over at Ledarius to make sure he was alright and not about to give a public display of "this nigga scared." The C.U.B.S spokesman was reciting the homicide statistics in Chicago when Quan and Stimey walked through the door in all black. Quan shook hands with Mr. Collins who had grown up in the neighborhood with his Uncle Deno over on Marshfield. He had caught a case for shooting a dude at Marshfield Park back when he was a teenager, he got out and moved to Milwaukee and turned his life around. He was there in support of the C.U.B.S organization to help the kids get off the streets, being from the streets himself, those who knew him still had respect and that gave Miss Freeman's effort even more credibility.

Marcus brought his adorable young daughter Iyana to the event, and Brooklyn and the rest of the girls went bananas. She had a full head of sandy beige hair and big brown eyes complete with a youthful spark of innocence. AK walked over and gave Iyana a big hug along with everybody else. "Hey Iyana, you are so pretty girl! What do you wanna be when you grow up?" Alikah asked her.

"A doctor." Iyana replied to the sounds of approval from everybody around that heard her.

"I wanna be a doctor so I can fix Andre's face." she said, and everybody died laughing. "Oh, why you gone do me like that?" AK said feeling slightly embarrassed, but shook off the diss like a champ and told her that he hopes that she accomplishes that one day. He gave her a hug and then him and the boys turned and left.

The girls swept Iyana up and took her off with them which gave Marcus time to check on how things were shaping up. Ledarius watched from across the room as his younger brother Quan was standing there with AK and Tick laughing and talking all buddy-buddy like. Ledarius felt his heartbeat accelerate at the sight but tried not to panic. Ledarius

200

would never tell Quan about any of the problems he was having knowing how Quan might react.

"Is that your brother over there Ledarius?" Marcus asked as he walked over and gave Dajon a fist bump and then sat down in the chair next to him, waiting for Ledarius to answer. "Your brother has a reputation Ledarius for being really dangerous and I don't want any trouble jumping off with all these kids around." Marcus gave Ledarius the look people give you when they trying to tell you something. "My brother is not dangerous." Ledarius replied feeling slightly bothered but also cautious.

"Okay, you a good kid Ledarius so I'm a trust you to keep things under control." Marcus said grabbing Ledarius on the shoulder to emphasize his point. Marcus meant well and Ledarius liked him. He looked over at his younger brother who he spent most of his life with and hated the fact that people always thought that he was going to start trouble and judged him based on hearsay, to Ledarius he was just his brother.

Cali jumped on the mic and talked through a bunch of feedback and then she introduced the first group of dancers. They were called the "Little Ri Ri's" and were in the five to twelve age group and were literally the cutest things you ever seen. They had on little costumes and face paint and had the audacity to come out dancing to Rihanna's work, work, work, work song. The bass was heavy, and the beat filled the entire room which was full of people cheering as the little divas danced their hearts out.

Brooklyn had finally made her way over to check on Ledarius and give him a kiss "Hey, little dragon boy." she said softly in his ear before biting his earlobe playfully and then kissing him again.

"Get a room you two." Dajon said sounding playfully annoyed. Alikah had come over to get Brooklyn and drag her away from Ledarius.

"You ever noticed how fine Alikah is? That smooth chocolate skin is so shiny, like damn." AK said discretely to Tick as he watched Alikah walk across the gymnasium back towards the stage. "Yeah, them African girls is the real queens, Nigerian, Guyanese and Ethiopian girls," Tick said in agreement. "Yeah, Ethiopian girls are Goddesses." Fang said as if he had just made a huge discovery.

The DJ spent Juice World, G Herbo and all the new young emerging Chicago talent, and then he slowed things down to get ready for the next dancers which was Brooklyn and her girls. They came out to Kanye West's song *"Monster"* and all the girls went nuts and Brooklyn performed it like she was born to dance. Her every move captivated everybody that was watching, she knew she was killing it, with Alikah, Vanessa and the twins hitting every move right along with her, the people on watching on the live stream just knew that they were witnessing a star in the making.

Dajon and Bug were clowning around and dancing along, enjoying themselves while Ledarius watched Brooklyn in awe of just how beautiful and talented she was. Seeing her move her body to the beat and her facial expressions that went from unbothered to fierce instantly. Her interpretation was electric with her movements ticking perfectly in sync with every drum kick and snare, the kids held their phones up recording the performance for their social media.

Brooklyn's performance was a big deal and the twins who were the lowkey life of the dance group, all got their usual praise with Vanessa and Alikah holding their own. Brooklyn felt a huge sense of accomplishment and relief as she jumped off stage and headed over to her man. They kissed and she held on to him and looked him in his eyes, then she abruptly stopped herself from getting what she described as hot and bothered.

Then Quan and Stimey came over and hung out with Ledarius for a couple of minutes just to announce that they had to go. Brooklyn, Cali and Alikah were spending the night at Brooklyn's and Vanessa and the twins were planning to link with Tick and the boys at AK's later. Marcus was responsible for the breakdown of the event, so he had his sister take Iyana home with her and he enlisted Ledarius and a few others to help out so they could get done in time to catch the fireworks.

Dajon and Bug stayed behind to help get the trash and pull down the decorations until their rides came to pick them up. Ledarius broke down the tables and chairs, then he set the trash bags by the back door so he could run them to the dumpster when he was finished. He finally got everything broken down and gathered all the trash to be thrown away.

He looked around for a doorstop to put in the door so he wouldn't get locked out, because then he would have to walk all the way around to the front door to get back in. Ledarius wasn't able to find the doorstop, so settled for a little trashcan he found to put in the door, and then he grabbed everything that needed to go and went out back.

35.

Play Time

"Whole heartedly, is you trying to be clever nigga?" -
Moochie

The sun had just begun to set and there were streaks of red and orange in the sky. The ground was wet as if a quick rain had come and gone to provide a little moisture to the heat. The air smelled like sulfur and the quietness of the alley gave an earie vibe. Ledarius threw the cardboard in the dumpster and then he threw the trash bags on top of them to weigh them down. He thought about if the trashcan somehow moved and the door closed, he'd be locked out, then he heard a sound and turned around to check. He didn't see anything, it must have been a cat, then he threw the last bag in the dumpster and when he turned around again, AK was standing right in front of him.

"Play time is over Ledarius!" AK said in the voice of his overly aggressive alter ego Damn Straight. "I'm about to beat the bitch outta you," he added. AK had it in his mind that Ledarius had some bitch in him, and that AK would actually be doing him a favor, if he beat it out of him.

Ledarius didn't know what to do and then Tick kicked the trashcan holding the door open and it slowly closed shut, and they all heard the sound of the lock when it clicked. AK pulled off his shirt and threw it on the ground. "You should thank me," he said pulling off his tank top like he was on a prison yard and throwing it down near where the shirt was. "You should thank me for beating the bitch out of you!" AK circled Ledarius like a lion in the jungle stalking his prey.

"Ledarius, Ledarius, Ledarius, I'm about to give you the kind of ass whooping that you gone remember when you old." AK said while Tick held the phone up to record everything, and Maine and Psyke guarded the perimeter. "Did Brooklyn tell you about us?" AK asked him, sensing that the provoking needed to be cranked up a notch. "Ask her about the jackhammer," he said with the most devilish smirk on his face and then he bit his own bottom lip. Ledarius had fire in his eyes.

"I don't see why Master Yang favor you so much." AK cracked his knuckles and then he cracked his own neck.

"Well, you're about to find out," Ledarius said finally standing up for himself as he pulled his shirt off and settled into his fighting stance. "Yeah Ledarius, come get this ass whooping," AK said and lunged forward.

Meanwhile, back on the block, Quan and Redrum were dropping off Stimey and heading towards Quan's grandmother's house to drop him off so he could make a play right quick and grab Gigi, then they were all supposed to meet back up in an hour. Quan went inside grannies to his secret spot and grabbed some of the work and tip toed back out the house, but as he was leaving, Moochie and his goons pulled up.

Two niggas jumped out the car and Quan tried to take off running, but he didn't make it far. They grabbed him and threw him in the back seat and Moochie turned around with a big ass smile on his face. Bruza hit the gas and they took off towards 85th.

They bent the corner and headed towards Hermitage. "You disappoint me, DeQuan. You let a low life thieving ass nigga in the circle of trust. Now, I can respect a hustler. Hell, I can even respect a nigga that kills people for a living, but I do not respect a thief, DeQuan." Moochie said with the utmost disgust in his voice.

"I agree whole heartedly." Quan responded with just the slightest touch of sarcasm in his voice, and that little bit was enough to piss Moochie off.

"Whole heartedly? Is you trying to be clever, nigga? You trying to be clever you little muthafucka." He put the pistol to Quan's head and pushed down on it hard so that it hurt. "Say something else clever muthafucka, I dare you little nigga." He had half of his body in the front passenger seat and the other half in the back seat with his hand around Quan's neck, with the pistol in the other hand pointed at his head. "I can't think of nothing." Quan responded honestly, but when Bruza chuckled in the front seat, it made it seem like Quan was still trying to be funny. "Muthafucka," Moochie tried to strangle Quan and smash his head open, but Quan was in the back seat of an 83 Chevy Caprice Classic, and those back seats are soft, so him trying to bang Quan's head against a soft seat wasn't really doing the damage he wanted. That frustrated him, so he just gave up and sat back in the front seat.

"Take this muthafucka to the big house." Moochie told Bruza and he turned the car around. Moochie had several places where he laid his head for different reasons. The big house was a house Moochie had inherited from his grandmother and he turned it into his fortress. Quan started to get concerned because he had heard stories about things that went on in that house and none of them ended good. To add insult to injury it was out in the 100's and he had no way of contacting anybody.

Meanwhile, in the alley behind the recreation center. "I'm about to make you bleed Ledarius, yeah that's right, even more than you already do once a month when you get your period." AK roared in his Damn Straight voice and then he attacked.

Ledarius was in trouble, AK was bigger and stronger, they exchanged blows, then Ledarius switched his style and caught AK with a few unexpected punches, momentarily stunning him.

"Aww I see you got some tricks up your sleeve huh?" AK commented running his tongue over his bottom lip to check and see how bad it was busted, and then he reset into his fighting stance, "Is that all you got?" He yelled out, and went after Ledarius again, and again Ledarius was too quick and wrapped AK up and kicked him in the mid-section as hard as he could, sending him flying backwards, AK looked confused for a second.

While Ledarius was fighting his case and was no longer attending the martial arts classes, that the judicial system felt turned him into the weapon that caused someone to become almost fatally injured. Master

Yang had a friend name Lin Wong who was up in age and needed some assistance with a gardening project at her home and Master Yang sent Ledarius over to help.

Lin Wong showed Ledarius a style that she called soft hand, it may have been a coincidence that the weekend before, Ledarius had spent the weekend over at Aunt Linda's and spent most of the time with his friend Snacks who turned Ledarius on to a movie called IP Man, about the Legendary Master Yip who went on to train the great Bruce Lee.

What began as a few lessons turned into a full one on one crash course in the discipline known as Wing Chun and Ledarius was using it now for the first time. "Yeah, that's what I'm talking about Ledarius." AK yelled and attacked Ledarius, who countered with quick rapid-fire punches, but AK had made the adjustments and caught Ledarius with some quick hard punches of his own hurting Ledarius and then AK picked him up and threw him against the dumpster.

"You better start glowing Jet Ledarius." AK yelled as he continued to attack Ledarius with savage intent. "You better start glowing real quick Ledarius cause this shit finna hurt boy." He hit Ledarius with a combination of hard punches then he grabbed his wrist and twisted it and flipped Ledarius over on his back knocking the wind out of him. He was about to put Ledarius in an arm bar, but he slipped out just in time. Tick moved in closer with his phone to make sure he was getting the best angle on the action while Maine and Psyke had to multitask by watching the fight while still being the lookouts.

AK slammed Ledarius against the dumpster again and put him in a head lock and started choking Ledarius until he was almost about to lose consciousness. Ledarius began to have flashbacks about all the times AK had disrespected and humiliated him and then the picture of him and Brooklyn entered his head. He thought about how AK said to ask her about his jackhammer and Ledarius got charged up and lifted his legs up in the air and brought them down and was able to break AK's hold on him.

Then Ledarius finally got a hold of himself. He attacked AK and began to do some real damage. He hit him with a flurry of punches from all angles and for the first time he had really hurt him, and he had no intention of letting up. He finally was able to catch AK and then he flipped him over and punched AK as hard as he could and almost knocked him out cold. Ledarius looked down at AK laid out on the ground appearing to be unconscious, finally, all the tough talk and crazy bravado was silenced.

Ledarius was bleeding in several places and was pretty sure he had some broken ribs; he was still recovering from just having the wind knocked out of him. In the last exchange he had went all out and had finally hurt AK who was now laid out on the concrete. Ledarius was relieved until he saw AK look at him and smile, then he spit a glob of blood out of his mouth. AK sprung back up to his feet and it seemed as if he was just getting started and was ready to go at Ledarius again, Ledarius didn't care either way, he knew what he had to do, it was situations like this that led to people getting killed or worse.

Then suddenly, Boom!! Boom!! Boom!! Boom!! Boom!! Boom!! Boom!! The sound of gun shots rang out causing everyone to freeze in their tracks. "Oh shit!" Tick shouted looking confused. "That shit sounded close," Psyke said with the same puzzled look on his face that matched the rest of them. They all looked around at each other as if the fight they were just having had never happened. AK and Tick started walking out towards where the gun shots had come from.

Ledarius followed behind, because what else was he supposed to do? When they walked around to the front of the Rec, they could immediately see the red and blue police lights at the entrance of the parking lot. "Oh shit!" Maine said underneath his breath, but everybody heard him. Then they all began to walk towards the commotion.

There was a grey Dodge Charger at the entrance of the parking lot with the horn blowing. The feeling of dread filled the boys as they walked around to get a closer look. To their horror, they came to the discover that it was Marcus, he was slumped over in the front seat of his car with his eyes open, dead.

A woman in the distance started screaming and pointing her finger "They shot him! Them muthafuckas shot that boy for nothing." The lady screamed hysterically and got her phone out and began yelling at the top of her lungs to somebody telling them what she saw. The police were trying to calm the angry crowd of people.

"Oh fuck!" Maine said as he looked and saw that Ms. Freeman coming to check on what was going on. When she saw Marcus's car, she went ballistic and started screaming and crying uncontrollably. "Marcus…Marcus," she screamed and fell to the ground. Tick and Psyke ran over to try and console her, then the rest of the staff that was still there all began to come out.

"Get out of here Ledarius! It ain't safe out here for us right now." AK told Ledarius and the boys vanished into thin air. Ledarius was still badly hurt from the fight he just had with AK, but was now traumatized by the sight of Marcus's lifeless body sitting up in the front seat of his car covered in blood. He made it to the bus stop and caught the bus just as it was about to pull off. He sat down and immediately felt the sting of fractured ribs and the pain of several scrapes and bruises.

Ledarius, had finally made it to the block, he got off the bus and crossed the street towards his house when he spotted a girl walking quickly in his direction. When the girl got up close to him, he recognized that it was Gigi and immediately knew that something was wrong, and when she started rambling, he definitely knew that something was wrong. Ledarius felt his heart drop from his chest, he just knew that she was about to tell him that something happened to his brother.

"Ledarius, Moochie took Quan. I was coming to meet up with him, and I was walking towards your grandmother's house, and I saw Moochie and them pull up, jump out and chase Quan into Aunt Evelyn's drive way, they jumped on him and put him in the car," she explained and as soon as the words left her mouth she started freaking out. "Calm down, Gigi." Ledarius told her trying to calm her down because she was about to make him start panicking along with her.

Ledarius panicked and started pacing back and forth for a minute and then he stopped and pulled out his phone. He thought about calling the police and then he thought about whether his mother knew. He went upstairs to check on his mother and found her knocked out on the couch. He turned around and slipped back out the door as quietly as he could.

He walked back and forth for a minute trying to gather his thoughts, then he decided to call Brooklyn. "Hello, hey, I need help, my brother is in trouble. He has been abducted by someone, I think. Can you please call Vanessa and see if she can come get you and bring you to me so that I can go and look for him?" Ledarius asked desperately. "Okay, okay, okay, wait, where are you?" Brooklyn asked sounding worried. "I'm in front of my apartment." Ledarius replied. "Okay, wait right there. I will be there in twenty minutes, don't leave." Brooklyn said and clicked off.

Ledarius thought about anyone else he could call, then a hooded figure appeared from around the corner and started coming towards him. Ledarius didn't know what to expect, but at that point he was ready for anything. The shady figure pulled the hoodie back revealing his face. It was Stimey, with the grey book bag he always kept. He told Gigi to go and try to find out anything that she could about where they could be holding Quan and hit him back with the business Asap Rocky. He looked at Ledarius and telepathically communicated everything he needed to know. He circled around him and put his back against the wall and kicked his foot up against it, then he pulled out a blunt he had rolled up and lit it without saying so much as a word and waited, because what was understood, did not need to be explained.

They waited for what seemed like an eternity and then a black and red escalade pulled up, and when the window rolled down, Ledarius almost lost it when he saw AK behind the wheel. "Let's go get your brother." AK looked at Ledarius. Stimey who was not much for hesitation walked right up to the mother ship, opened the door and jumped in. Ledarius after that point had no choice but to get in, he looked at AK one more time and reluctantly got in behind Stimey.

When Ledarius called Brooklyn and told her what happened to Quan, Brooklyn panicked and called Vanessa to see if she could get the car and come and pick her up and take her over to Ledarius, but when she called Vanessa, she was with the twins at AK's house. When AK overheard the conversation, he thought about how much he had just beat the shit out of Ledarius, who had to still be hurting and now somebody just snatched his brother, that had to be rough and after a few hits of the rose bud and a few seconds of recollection, AK got up.

It was surreal for Ledarius to be actually riding in the vehicle that carried his tormentors in and out of his life for the past month, not to mention that he was sitting directly behind the ringleader himself. Tick was sitting in the passenger seat with Maine sitting on the other side of Stimey. There was an awkward silence inside the car for a minute until Tick reached back and passed the blunt to Ledarius. "He don't want that." Stimey said and took the blunt out of Tick's hand and hit it.

They pulled up to a three flat apartment at an undisclosed location and descended from the mother ship. They entered a front door and then another door and ascended to the top floor where they entered, yet another door. AK's apartment was big and plushed out, he had a big 65-inch TV in the living room, and everything in the house was color coordinated with the black, red and white colors of the brotherhood, and there were even two full wall murals of the B.O.A insignia. The walls

214

were lined with bookshelves full of books of all sorts. "I got books in here that the government would be mad about." AK stated when he noticed Ledarius looking. He had a computer room with what seemed to be spy equipment in there and a danger room with various kinds of exercise equipment. Inside his kitchen they had containers filled with natural herbs and jars of fermented vegetables infused with all sorts of things that heal and strengthen the body.

The boys were putting on all black ninja gear that had the B.O.A symbol somewhere on it. AK walked Ledarius into another room that you had to enter through a trick door built into the kitchen pantry. The room was full of weapons of all kinds, from ninja weapons to handguns and all sorts of cool gadgets and tactical gear. AK turned the light on. "Go ahead Ledarius, pick out whatever you need," he insisted.

36.

The Mission

"Aww, you ain't said shit slick to a can of oil" - Moochie

Quan was tied to a chair in a basement way out in the hundreds, with no way of contacting anyone to let them know his whereabouts. The Big House was where Moochie felt the safest, not only because most people that he dealt with had no idea where the spot was. But those that did, knew that Moochie had a small army of shooters over there that were ready to handle anything that popped off.

Moochie sat at a table in a chair on the opposite side of Quan. Bruza was sitting across from them sharpening a hunting knife. One of Moochie's soldiers came from upstairs and whispered something in his ear. Moochie sat back in his chair and stared at Quan as if he was deciding what to do with him. "How do I know that you and him wasn't planning to rob me this whole time?" Moochie was sipping on a bottle of Remy Martin, never once taking his eyes off Quan.

"Cause I ain't stupid, and you know I don't steal shit! Plus, if I was gon' steal some shit, Joe, I would have took everything." Quan pulled on the duct tape that had his hands bound to the back of the chair. "Let me go Moochie." Quan said as he pulled on the duct tape again, but it was no use. "If I was to let you go, you and them little fuckers would just want revenge." Moochie sat up in his chair and looked at Quan. "Wouldn't you?" he asked as he grabbed a pack of Newport 100's off the table and pulled one out and lit it.

"So, what you finna do then?" Quan replied as his fear slowly began to turn into anger. "Kill me?" Moochie let a slight grin form on his face. When he did that the fear began to creep back in and Quan started to sweat. Moochie knew that if he let Quan go, he would begin plotting against him and that wasn't a risk he was willing to take.

Stimey got off his phone with Gigi who said she had spoken to Redrum, who said he had hollered at a few of the guys and found out that they were holding Quan at the Big House. Ledarius wasn't worried about going to war with a known drug dealer with a reputation for torture and murder. No, Ledarius was worried about his brother, and what would happen if his mom found out something bad had happened to him.

They were riding in a black-on-black Dodge Durango, minus the B.O.A emblem and equipped with a police scanner and a few other added gadgets. The B.O.A code of conduct forbid them from smoking while conducting any type of official business, so the ride out there was fairly quiet. The GPS said they were twelve minutes away. Stimey being the only one who had ever actually been to the big house had drawn a full layout of the house and the surrounding landmarks.

AK hung up the phone with the Shiite who was strategically posted nearby just in case there were any unforeseen circumstances. Ledarius was in the back seat rubbing his fingertips together, he was amazed by what the sodium hydroxide AK told him to apply to temporarily remove his fingerprints felt like. The GPS said they were two minutes away.

Maniac was posted on one end of the block and Psycho was posted on the other end of the block, both of them strapped with enough fire power to neutralize anything coming their way. AK, Ledarius, Tick and Stimey would make the extraction. The GPS said one minute away. They turned on to the street and drove at a moderate pace. There were people outside on their front porches and a bunch of niggas in the streets, drinking and smoking and talking shit. There were a few kids out still trying to get the last little bit of fireworks out of their systems.

"Your destination is on the left," announced the voice on the GPS, but they rolled past so they could circle the block and pull up in the alley. When they got there, Tick shot something that wasn't a gun at the streetlight in the alley and it knocked the light out, turning the alley completely dark. They pulled a few houses up past the big house and parked, then Tick got out of the car and disappeared, literally.

Meanwhile, in the basement, Quan had just got punched in the face by Moochie for getting smart with him again. He spit some blood out of his mouth and tried to relax because he had got a little light-headed and didn't want to pass out. Bruza was sitting in a chair behind Moochie smoking and taking sips off a mini bottle of Hennessey, simultaneously looking at Quan like he felt sorry for him and wanted to help him somehow, but he knew there was nothing that he could do.

"I'm gon' run outta patience with you real soon DeQuan, and you know ain't no letting you go, so you and the Rug Rats can plot treason against me." Moochie had also been hitting key bumps of cocaine out of a little blue bag for the past few hours and was starting to go from hot to cold without warning. Quan had gone through a range of emotions himself and was now beginning to reach his breaking point.

"You mean like the treason you committed against my pops?" Bruza's eyes lit up and Moochie's eyes got low and the look on his face showed what he was thinking. Anybody that was trying to stay alive probably wouldn't have said that, but Quan was tired and hungry and was starting not to give a fuck. "On my momma, my guy did time with your old celly Juice up in Joliet and he was singing like his name was Robert Sylvester and your name came up." Quan felt a jolt of courage come over him after the words came out his mouth.

"Is that right little nigga? You was always too resourceful for your own good." Moochie said and then he pulled out a big ass hunting knife with ridges on the blade and looked at Quan like he had plans of using it on him. "Yeah boy, way to resourceful for your own good," he repeated and then he dumped some of the cocaine from the little bag on to the tip of the knife and snorted it, then he looked at Quan with a wicked smile.

Tick opened the passenger side door and jumped back in and gave AK the nod. "Okay, everybody straight? Anybody got any concerns or reservations about this shit? Speak now or bury that shit down deep inside." AK said checking the temperature of everybody in the car before they got out. Seconds later he and Tick said something in another language underneath their breath that sounded something kind of like a prayer but there was no way of telling, the BOA was said to have developed another language where they could communicate with each other without outsiders being able to tell what they were saying.

People were popping firecrackers in the front while the boys were about to move in from the back. Stimey flicked his finger against the special Kevlar Vest he got from the danger room. Ledarius pulled the mask over his face, as did the rest of them and they hopped out the Durango and disappeared through the gate behind Moochies hideout.

AK told Tick to keep the perimeter clear and make sure nobody else enters the house. Tick pulled out twin desert eagles with silencers on them and disappeared into the darkness. AK, Ledarius and Stimey snuck around the side of the house as firecrackers in the front popped off at random intervals. They went down the back steps and listened at the back door to try to hear what was going on inside.

Moochie had sat the hunting knife down on the table to smoke another square and talk some more shit to Quan while he decided his fate. Bruza leaned back in his chair and started checking his text messages. Something inside of Quan snapped. "If you finna kill me after all the shit I did for you then go ahead then, kill me." Quan got heated and if looks could kill Moochie would be a goner. "Aww you ain't said shit slick to a can of oil little nigga." Moochie replied and put down his cigarette and picked up the hunting knife. Then they all looked up when they heard a light knock on the door. "Who the fuck?" Moochie put the knife down and grabbed his gun then Bruza went to the door and asked who is it?

Then suddenly the whole door got kicked off of the hinges and when Moochie tried to raise that gun to shoot, a throwing knife hit him right in the shoulder blade and he dropped the gun. Ledarius flew in through the doorway and kicked Bruza over the table.

AK leaped in and began attacking Moochie's goons that ran downstairs when they heard all the commotion. Stimey ran right over to Quan and began to cut the duct tape with his box cutter. Quan's eyes had fire in them when he realized what was happening. Stimey got the duct tape off and then he stood up and turned around.

Quan jumped up out of the chair like a demon possessed and unzipped the gray book bag and reached inside pulling out two pistols and handed them to Stimey so smoothly that it seemed liked something they had done before. Without blinking, he reached back into the book bag and pulled out two more guns and yelled, "Chu wanna play rough?" in his Tony Montana voice. "Okay," he shouted and started shooting at Moochie, who had taken off running, trying to get away.

The guys outside that heard the gun shots started pulling out their pistols and coming over to see what was going on. Tick, with his desert eagles with the silencers on them was outside of the house keeping the perimeter clear, and by keeping the perimeter clear, I mean he was popping whoever entered his general proximity. Tick was a highly skilled marksmen, and swung his guns like a ninja does his swords, he called it Gun fu.

Tick was like Leon in the movie *The Professional*, the way he suddenly appeared out of the darkness, hit his target with one shot, and disappeared back into the darkness. He moved like a ghost and niggas was dropping like flies and never even knew where the shots were coming from, Psst! Psst! Psst! was all you heard.

A couple of Moochie's guys were scrambling around the house with their pistols out, when one of them thought he saw Tick, but when he raised his gun to shoot, Tick had disappeared. They called a couple more soldiers over to help, but, when they ran over, one of them felt an itch in his chest and when he looked down, he saw the blood and then he fell to the ground and then, two of the dudes next to him fell out the same way.

The other guys just started shooting all wild at nothing, then they charged in blindly and Tick picked them off too. Dudes were running everywhere and when they thought they had finally got the drop on him, Tick threw a smoke bomb on the ground and disappeared into a puff of white smoke. They were like damn what the fuck, then two silent shots came through the cloud of smoke, and they suddenly dropped to the ground.

Ledarius and AK fought their way up the stairs from the basement leaving broken bodies the whole way. They fought side by side as if they weren't just fighting each other a few hours before. Ledarius whipped out a pair of nunchucks and began whooping muthafuckas asses with them so thoroughly that AK had to stop and admire his skills for a second. But then, a big 200-pound goon rushed him, and AK broke him down and then slammed him through the kitchen table.

Moochie's soldiers were startled when they saw three of their homeboys just drop dead, without seeing who shot them. One of the dudes thought he saw where Tick was and ran over towards where he thought he saw him, but just as they got close, Tick threw a second smoke bomb and disappeared again, and as their eyes adjusted to what they were seeing, Tick squeezed off a few more quick shots through the smoke and they both dropped the same way the others had.

Moochie ran towards the front door with DeQuan right on his tail and Stimey not too far behind him. Quan let off three more shots at him and then took off through the door after him. He hopped over the banister right on Moochie's tracks. Stimey ran out the house and jumped over the banister just like Quan did and landed on his feet and took off behind him. Moochie reached his Chevy and hurried up trying to get his keys out and open the door.

He jumped in and put the key in the ignition and started that bitch up and pulled out into the street. Quan saw him and began chasing the car on foot, running beside it on the sidewalk. Psyke was at the end of the block to make sure nothing got in or out. Quan with Stimey right on his heels in one swift motion went off the sidewalk through the grass and in between two cars and was suddenly on the side of Moochie's car in the street.

Moochie looked to his left and saw Quan and then almost in slow motion he saw the pistol. Quan squeezed off five rounds hitting Moochie in the head. Moochie's car swerved into a parked car and came to a loud screeching halt. Quan walked up to Moochie's window and shot him two more times. Quan turned around and cut back through the parked cars, back towards the house. Stimey walked up after Quan had turned and left and fired off six more rounds into Moochie's lifeless body and then looked around for a second and then took off behind Quan.

223

Quan saw Ledarius waiting for him outside, so he ran over to him and Ledarius signaled for him to go get in the truck. On the way to the truck with Stimey and Ledarius right behind him, he ran right into Bruza. Bruza threw his hands in the air and gave Quan the *yeah, I'm still hard but please don't kill me* look. Quan aimed the pistol at his head about to pull the trigger but decided at the last second not to. "Go ahead Bruza, you the general now." Quan told him and turned and headed for the truck. "Ayye you got a job." Stimey told Bruza as he passed by him imitating the famous scene from Scarface and headed off behind Quan with Ledarius behind them.

They jumped in the truck with AK and Tick already waiting in the front seats and Stimey jumped in the back. They pulled off slowly and headed for the expressway with the 4th of July fireworks still going off in the background. AK said it was better to move slow but steadily because people always remember the vehicle that they saw speeding away, but they never remember the car that rolled casually away from the scene, because it never stuck out in their memory.

The scene around the big house looked like a massacre had taken place with bodies and bullet holes everywhere. AK hung the phone up letting the Shiite know they had made a safe exit, then he checked the rearview mirror to make sure that Psyke and Maine were behind them. Everyone in the car was quiet and the awkward silence was making things uncomfortable.

Ledarius looked over at Quan, and Quan looked back at him. "You shot somebody tonight." He finally managed to say to his younger brother who seemed the least bit bothered. "Man, I done shot a lot of muthafuckas Ledarius." Quan responded annoyed but everybody else in the car found it funny and burst into laughter, which broke the tension. "You fucking with my Fung Shui right now Ledarius, let me tell you," Quan said to even more laughter from AK and Tick, and Stimey in the back.

They rode back to town and dropped Stimey off at his house, and then went to drop off Ledarius and Quan. When they pulled up AK got out the car to talk to Ledarius. Quan gave Tick dap and jumped out and gave AK a solid handshake. "Yo', much gratitude my guy." Quan said looking AK in the eye to show how serious he was about him coming to help his brother come save him. "I'm 'bout to go in the house and wait for this guy to go to sleep so I can turn on Porn Hub and knock myself out." Quan added and turned and made his way into the house.

AK stood in front of Ledarius and put out his hand. "You fought good tonight, Jet Li Darius," he said with sincerity. "So, who is the Master then?" Ledarius asked being funny but also wanting to know what was next. "Ledarius, the way they doing us out here, we need all the Master's we can get, you feel me?" He shook his hand again and pulled him in for the bro hug and walked back to the car. "Until we meet again Jet Li Darius," he said and jumped back in the truck and gave Ledarius a salute, and then him and Tick pulled off. Ledarius went up the stairs as Quan was opening the front door.

"Hey, what y'all doing?" they heard Cynthia holler through the door from her bedroom. "Nothing," they both answered simultaneously and headed to their room and closed the door. Cynthia laid back down feeling the comfort a mother feels when her boys make it home safe in a city where so many mothers have nightmares with the stress of having young sons who never make it home out the streets.

37.

The Beginning

"Decalcify your pineal gland" - Tick

"Y"ou know it's time to get 'em on…No doubt about it we getting scummy…you know we get 'em up early but we got 'em scummy"

"You know it's time to get 'em ooon…No doubt about it we getting scummy…you know we get 'em up early but we got 'em scummy"

The DJ that night was mixing an acapella version of the Chi Town Anthem, "Scummy" by the one and only Crucial Conflict. He did that for a minute to tease the crowd and then he let that beat drop and the energy was electric. The multicolored lights in the club that night created just the right atmosphere and the heavy bass coming out of the speakers created just the right vibration. The girls had their hair and nails done and they were putting Victoria secret models to shame. The guys all made sure that every stitch of clothing they had on was sharp and crisp.

Mr. Gene owned Mr. G's Supperclub & Entertainment Center and was a man of respect, so most niggas knew not to come up in there with that bullshit. Tonight, was a special night, because tonight was the big Chicago's Got Talent Showcase. WGCI was there streaming the event live on their website and all the hottest artist in the city that had gotten chosen to perform was ready to bring they entire movement to the big stage.

87th street was lit up with bright lights and a red carpet with big expensive media cameras flashing away. The line outside was full of beautiful people who came dressed to impress and ready to take all the high-profile pics they could to prove it. The event was all ages so there was no alcohol being served, but the ballers who had money knew how to get what they wanted brought in and wasn't nobody gone really press the issue as long as they kept it out of sight.

Tonight was the night Cali had been waiting for. She and the girls were sitting in the parking lot smoking Rose Bud in Vanessa's sugar daddy's whip listening to Sasha Go Hard. They all had on Chicago Bulls jerseys because nothing was more Chicago, than the Chicago Bulls. Cali had on a black and red Derrick Rose #1 and Brooklyn had on the Joakim Noah #13 jersey. The rest of the girls all had on the white and red Jordan #23 jerseys, which had them all looking like how Da Brat used to dress back in the 90's. Cali rolled down the window to holler at a group of people walking in, letting them know to fuck wit' her on the gas. Cali blew her smoke out through the sunroof and passed the blunt to Brooklyn who was still doing her make up in the mirror and singing along to Sasha Go Hard. Brooklyn hit the blunt and passed it back and finished doing her make up. Cali randomly screamed out at the top of her lungs channeling her energy. Then they opened the doors and exited the vehicle like celebrities and walked straight up to the front door and was let right through. AK had purchased two VIP sections and had things moved around until it was one big VIP section. AK, Tick. Maine, Psyke and Fang were already there when Cali, Brooklyn, Alikah, Vanessa, Camisha and Teneshia walked up looking like baddies.

The boys were on one side of the VIP and the girls had settled in on the other side talking amongst themselves. Brooklyn looked up and smiled the brightest smile ever at Ledarius, who was standing across the room holding a bouquet of roses. Brooklyn blushed for a second and then she sailed across the VIP, into his arms. They hugged and stared into each other's eyes and kissed.

Then Brooklyn and Ledarius both looked over at AK and Alikah, who were also hugged up together, and were now trying to steal all "the new couple alert" shine. Ledarius walked over and him and AK hugged and stood together talking with their girls by their sides.

Dajon made a grand entrance holding up the acceptance letter into the accelerated Math program at Kennedy King College the next semester. He danced up wearing the black and red Rajon Rondo Chicago Bulls number 9 jersey with the black and red Jordan's to match. The DJ dropped a new record by Dreezy and that shit went crazy instantly. He walked up and hugged Ledarius and went and gave AK dap and Tick and Maine and Psyke and Fang and then went over and got hugs and love from all the girls while his cousin was getting into her zone.

Quan and Stimey slipped in from the side of the VIP when no one had even seen them come through the front door. They were dressed in all black except for the diamonds in their ears and the jewelry on their necks and wrist. They gave dap to everybody and posted up on the back of the couches with their feet in the seats. The twins were sitting with Psyke and Maine, and Vanessa had been flirting with Fang all night.

Cali came over to break up all that boo'd up shit and took Alikah and Brooklyn with her to go and give the DJ her music, and also because Alikah needed to make sure that she could plug her laptop in to make sure she could play the video that went along with Cali's performance that she had just stayed up all night until 3 o'clock in the morning editing. The DJ put on that King Louie and shouted him out like he might be in the building.

Ledarius and AK sat down and looked out at everybody in the club kicking it, trying to either choose or get chose, then AK winced a little bit and grabbed his rib. "Hey, my back still hurt from when you kicked me up against that dumpster ghat dammit." AK confessed to Ledarius in a moment of transparency. "Well, my back and my elbows still hurt from when you dragged me on the ground and my skin got scraped off, and now every time I get in the shower and the hot water hit it, it stings a little." AK started laughing and Ledarius laughed along with him.

"What's the last book you read Ledarius?" AK asked as he lit the blunt that Alikah had just rolled up and passed to him.

"I'm almost finished with *The Mandrake*." Ledarius responded looking over to see where Brooklyn was.

"Niccolo huh? Mr. Machiavelli himself, good one." AK replied impressed. "Interesting fella that guy." He hit the blunt and leaned his head back and blew out a big cloud into the air.

He passed the blunt to Ledarius and Ledarius refused of course and respectfully declined. "Go ahead Ledarius and unblock your chakras." AK told him jokingly. "Yeah, come on Ledarius decalcify yo' pineal gland." Tick playfully shot at him in his Smokey from Friday voice. Tick was actually creating a new strand of marijuana infused with Ormus Gold that he felt could actually decalcify a person's Pineal Gland. Ledarius looked around a couple of times and finally said fuck it, he took the blunt and put it to his lips and inhaled.

Ledarius was choking his lungs out while everybody was looking at him with smiles on their faces. Ledarius choked some more, and Tick saw that it was good. "It's okay, it's okay. You supposed to choke, it opens the capillaries." he told him with amusement. Quan looked at his brother in utter disbelief, cause in all his years he had never once ever seen his brother even remotely close to looking like he wanted to hit a blunt, let alone be doing it.

"What other books have you read Ledarius? How old were you when you first read *The Art of War*." AK asked finally able to vibe with another reader on the same level as him. "I was thirteen or fourteen," Ledarius answered feeling a little bit like a nerd.

"I was twelve," AK laughed out. "I bullshit you not bro," he laughed again. "I was eleven when I began deciphering ancient Sumerian text." AK hit the blunt again and held in the smoke and took a drink of

Pineapple juice. The brethren had strict laws against drinking alcohol, after he hit the blunt again, he blew the smoke out into the air.

"What about the 48 laws?" he asked Ledarius already expecting the answer knowing pretty much that that's an easy one for a reader of a certain level.

"Oh yeah," Ledarius replied as he started to feel that wave when that first high starts to kick in.

"What about Mastery?" AK cracked his neck and his shoulders and took in a deep breath and sat back and hit the blunt again. "Yeah, go ahead and read everything by him. "What about *The Secret*?" AK like a swift hunter began to nudge Ledarius closer and closer to the rabbit hole.

"Oh yeah, I made my whole family read it." Ledarius laughed at the memory of Quan's face when he thought he had finally learned enough higher knowledge to become the Magneto of getting money, as he put it one night when Ledarius had suspected him of drinking too much Mountain Dew.

"Bingo!!" AK thought to himself let's go.

"What about *Behold a Pale*…hold that thought?" AK said and got up to shake hands with an old school rapper from the North Side of Chicago named E.C. ILLA and sat back down. "What about *Think and Grow Rich*?" AK threw him a curve ball, setting him up for the next pitch.

"Nah," Ledarius replied shaking his head and positioning his ear to catch what was coming next. "See, these dudes out here on the streets want money, but they lack the brains to really get it. I mean really really get it." AK waited for the server girl to leave before he finished.

"That's why the first principle of the Assassin Doctrine is self-mastery, particularly mastering your emotions. The reason these dudes out here going to jail all the time and dying is because they can't control their emotions. The root of all evil is not money Ledarius, its emotions, and that's why these dudes are caught in a continuous cycle of failure and negativity." AK checked his phone. "Your only supposed to allow an emotion to hit you and then move on, dwelling in emotions allows evil to seep its way into your being."

"Wait until you get to the sacred geometry." Maine teased.

"You just mad cause the sacred geometry was whooping yo 'ass." Psyke flipped it back on Maine.

"Everybody can't be like Tick." Fang said as Tick let a slight grin quickly appear on his face and then disappear.

"The lessons stack on top of each other, you'll get it." AK assured him. "We are Assassins Ledarius, of a sacred order, we have no political, religious or gang affiliation of any kind, after we take our oath, our only earthly loyalty is to the brotherhood and the doctrine that governs the covenant we stand upon.

"You know Tick is the one that came up with the no excuses policy, excuses are tools of the incompetent." AK hit the blunt and blew the smoke out. "I was once told Ledarius that a loser will always find an excuse to keep being a loser, but a winner always finds a way to win, be weary of those that always have excuses Ledarius." He looked at him for a second to see if his receivers were tuned in. "And that's what separates them from us, and that is why trying to save everyone is only a waste of time and an unnecessary risk.

"We cannot save everybody Ledarius because they don't wanna be saved, so let them continue to be the food that feeds the beast's belly. We will have no part of that, we only work towards the advancement of our own agenda. We will survive what's coming because we are aware of our higher purpose." AK hit the blunt again and past it to Ledarius which he usually never did. AK and the brethren usually didn't pass weed back and forth, everybody had their own blunt that they rolled and smoked, except for special occasions.

"They are consumed by ignorance Ledarius; they bathe in it," he commented and sipped his Pineapple juice and let out a little burp then he hit the blunt again. "They let same low vibrational shit be fed directly into their heads all day and wonder why they can't prosper and why they can't get it together, they are literally being fueled by ignorance." AK hit the blunt again.

"I am not fueled by ignorance Ledarius." AK looked at him.

"I'm fueled by God." he told Ledarius with a look in his eyes to let him know that he was deadly serious about what he was saying.

"See, what they don't understand is that you cannot ascend to the next level of consciousness to even begin to be able to manifest things into the physical realm if you are a stupid nigga, you just gon' keep losing over and over, but you can't tell them shit and that's why we keep the collective knowledge of the brotherhood strictly to the brethren, they would lose their fucking marbles if they knew what I knew." Dajon came and sat down next to Ledarius.

"They follow what they hear the next nigga say." He hit the blunt.

"I blame McDonald's." Tick said and cracked up laughing. "And rap music," he laughed, shaking hands with Jacob who had just walked up and gave Ledarius dap and sat down next to Dajon. "I don't listen to much new rap music. Well, I fuck with Kendrick, and I fuck with Lupe. He is definitely one of us." AK told Ledarius.

"We Assassins follow a code Ledarius, we believe in morals and integrity, and we understand the meaning of true selfless brotherhood, which is beyond a regular nigga's capacity to comprehend. Everybody wants individual power, because they don't understand that collective power is more formidable, and that's what every other race knows except for black people, and that's why black people are the only race still behind the poverty line."

The Brotherhood only works towards our own advancement, our own collective agenda." AK pulled out his phone and sent a quick text.

"Never trust a man that worships money Ledarius. He cannot be trusted. Never trust a man that will put pussy over the movement. I don't care how fine she is." AK got into his mode. Now, I'm not one of them guys that's disrespectful to women, because I truly understand the true beauty and essence of a woman. "The woman is the completion of power Ledarius, the Yin and the Yang. See, as a single man you are only able to access and utilize 360 degrees of knowledge, wisdom and understanding."

"But once you truly combine your energy with that right woman, then you are then able to access 720 degrees of knowledge wisdom and understanding and that's when the two of you combined can began to truly manifest your desires into reality, that's why she is referred to as the better half. That's what the separation agenda being pushed against our people is designed to keep under control, that true union. He put his fingers together and joined hands. "It's power in that spiritual union." He kissed Alikah as her and Brooklyn walked by to check on them.

"Watch, they will begin to attack love, in the movies we watch, and, in the music, we listen to. They started back with slavery selling off the spouses and breaking up the family structure, which leads to the breakup of the natural parental energy of a woman and man. Then the welfare system created the no man in the household policy that put our women in the situation they still suffer from today. Then in the early 90's, Snoop Dogg told the whole generation before us not to love or trust no woman, while the whole time he got a beautiful wife at home and healthy beautiful well-fed children, he was telling our fathers to say fuck a bitch; that brother really need to answer for that by the way."

"Now, this Love and Hip-Hop side chick/side nigga normalization gets introduced, so the whole household is separated from the start. As a microcosm, which translates directly to the whole neighborhood being separated, and that's how black kids get shot down in the streets and nobody does anything, because nobody is unified, disrespect is normalized because everybody is out for self.

"Do you know that when you master your emotions and master your impulses, you master your ability to block and filter bullshit, and when you combine that with a high intellectual capacity and God, you can access a frequency that directly correlates to being able to manifest your desires into the physical world?" AK looked at Ledarius who he could tell was absorbing everything. "You can't ascend to the next level

236

being bombarded with ignorance, it doesn't work that way." The show was about to start, but Cali had quite a few people ahead of her.

"Today, the cypher is complete Ledarius." AK said leaning in so that Ledarius over stood what he was saying. "Me..Tick..Maine..Psyke and Fang make five and my black book candidate that we will simply refer to as the Shiite make six and you make seven Ledarius." AK paused for dramatic effect. "And the brethren can only ascend to the next level, right now we can only ascend in multiples of seven Ledarius." Dajon looked over at AK with curiosity. "Today we are but seven, but one day there will be thousands." AK assured. "How many thousands?" Dajon asked with childlike sincerity then blurted out, "Hey I'm a numbers guy, what do you want from me?" he said in a faux Italian accent a man after Quan's own heart.

"One hundred and forty-four thousand," AK responded in a voice he rarely used and then repeated, as to really drive the point home. "One hundred and forty-four thousand Assassins, enlightened with God's grace and glory, wielding his divine permission to chop the wretched to pieces in a massacre of karma and retribution. I am the apex predator Ledarius, the arch assassin," he stared at Ledarius for a second to make sure that shit sunk in.

"That's what makes you so unique Ledarius." AK lowered his voice so only those two could hear. "Your total lack of ignorance and selfishness makes you a natural to ascend to the highest levels of consciousness and power, faster than most because you have the luxury of not having to unlearn a bunch of low frequency mindsets and subconsciously ingrained behavioral dysfunctions."

"It is you, that will bring balance to the brotherhood Ledarius, and when you reach that level of mental, physical and spiritual illumination, then you will truly experience "The Glow" Ledarius, and that my brethren is, God's light, and that is not an easy torch to bear, because those who cannot genetically achieve that level of enlightenment because of the limitations of their own kundalini, will hate you and try to kill and destroy you, and that is why the Assassin must always stay prepared to shed blood in the name of righteousness." Ledarius was becoming increasingly excited to begin his training which as far as he could tell, leaned heavy on a specific number of books every new initiate has to read in order to proceed to the following levels.

Ledarius was surprised when he saw his old friend Snacks. "What up Ledarius?" Snacks greeted him with a smile and a hug. "Yo', guess what? They dropped my case; I told them I wasn't trying to piss on no little kitten." The truth is Snacks really did try to piss on that kitten, and right now he was lying through his teeth as he would later admit, he said he just wanted to see if he could. The DJ played that Montana of 300, and that shit had the whole club on its feet.

Maine leaned over to AK and told him that he was cool with Ledarius and all, but to please leave him out of it the next time he decided to recruit somebody. They all laughed and shook hands. Cali was pacing back and forth mouthing her words silently to herself and getting into her mode before she was set to go on stage.

Brooklyn came over to check on Ledarius and kiss him, just because she just had to and there wasn't nothing he could do about it, and Alikah, took the que to go swap spit with AK real quick. The judges had finally arrived and were doing photo opps on the red carpet with influencers and local bloggers, while media outlets snapping away with these super expensive cameras. The judges were Chance the Rapper who always enjoyed the hometown love and Los Angeles R&B singer/Songwriter Ty Dolla $ign and Diamond from the Iconic Atlanta based rap group Crime Mob.

The host took the stage to announce the next act, he tapped the microphone. "Ladies and gentlemen, I would like for y'all to welcome Cali Capone to the stage, Cali Capone where you at?" Then Cali and the girls stood up, and passed the rest of the Rose Bud around and hurried up to the side of the stage. Drastik who had produced the beat that Cali was about to perform with was sitting in the section near the judges, because he was beginning to build a name for himself and plus him and Chance had some mutual friends in common. Cali jumped on stage and while she waited for the DJ to play the record. She addressed the crowd. "Yo' what up? Some of y'all may know me." Some dudes in the back screamed out her brother's name with a few R.I.P's added in there. "I'm DJ Sinister's sister," she choked up and cleared her throat. "And some of y'all may have even known my boy Marcus who was killed by the police at the Rec Center last week for no reason. We don't know what happened, but we do know that somebody ain't telling the truth." Some of the people in the audience shouted out the same sentiment.

"Well…it's time to let these crooked muthafuckas know that we the youth of the city and we tired of this killing us shit. Everybody in crowd yelled out in support of her statement. These muthafuckas need to know today that we ain't finna be silent. And these muthafuckas need to know that we the future of this city and you muthafuckas finna hear from us 'cause we got something to say, ghat dammit," and then the DJ dropped the beat and the baseline kicked in.

"R.I.P Marcus, love you fam." Cali shouted as the 808's kicked in and she went into her first verse. She rapped with a vengeance and not only did the ones who actually knew Marcus felt her, but even the ones who didn't know him, but was just sick of black boys dying period felt her to, and the energy level went up.

Cali bounced around the stage and captured the crowd in a way that caught everybody off guard. I mean, you can see a person freestyle and bullshit, but when you see somebody, you thought you knew do something so amazing that you never witnessed before, you be in shock like damn.

The video that Alikah had stayed up until 3 o'clock in the morning editing had finally began showing images of Marcus when he was little. There were pictures of him hugging his momma and smiling as he rode his first bicycle and flicks of him with a smile on his face sitting in a pile of toys on Christmas when he was kid. The energy went up another notch when the picture of him holding his newborn daughter Iyana flashed across the screen, followed by several pictures of her growing up being held in her daddy's arms. Some people in the crowd had tears in their eyes but were still jamming at the same time.

The judges were blown away and Diamond even stood up and rocked back and forth and threw her hands up in the air looking like a beautiful petite little hood goddess. The moment had an even deeper significance to Cali, not only was she really performing for the first time in front of people who could actually do something to help her career, but the idea for the video came from a movie that she remembered vaguely watching with her big brother with she was little.

In the movie the main characters best friend had been killed on the railroad tracks in New York and was electrocuted on the spot. Later in the movie the main character Kenny, who was also a DJ/Rapper, which was why her brother and her had gravitated to him, and his younger brother Lee, who was an awesome break dancer.

The movie was called Beat Street, and this was her Ramo moment. She fought to keep her emotions in check because she didn't wanna cry in front of everybody, so she channeled that energy and turnt the fuck up, and so did everybody else when she spit the line.

Feeling like Ice Cube, why they shoot my dude, got me in this bitch like Yo'

With my finger on the trigger, with a bunch of wild niggas, and we all in this bitch on Go

Got love for the fam, now we sitting like damn, cause we can't let 'em do us like this

Now, we all finna snap, and this ain't a fucking rap, cause we the youth of the city in this Bitch!!

Then she went into the hook of the song which repeated, "We the youth of the city Bitch," over and over and the whole club went bananas. The energy was electric, and the girls controlled the stage like pros. Cali had the room eating out of the palm of her hands with Brooklyn and the rest of the girls backing her up with their mesmerizing dance routine.

When the song was over Cali held her mic up in the air and received her praise from the crowd. She got a standing ovation from the crowd and the judges. Cali was definitely feeling the love from the room. She put the mic down and walked off the stage, and when she walked past the judges table Diamond waved her over.

Diamond stood up and gave Cali a big hug. "Girl, you did that," she said as she pulled out her phone and told Cali to take her info and to hit her up. "You want me to come to Atlanta?" Cali felt her dreams finally coming true. "Nah, we full." Diamond told her. When Cali looked disappointed, Diamond rescued her. "Yeah, sis hit me up, let's work." she playfully said, reassuring her. "Okay, bet. Thank you so much." Cali said giving her another hug before she left.

When Cali got back to the section, she was met with an outpouring of cheers and excitement from everybody, that was her confirmation, and she knew from that moment on what she wanted to do with her life. She got hugs from everybody, and even random waiters and waitresses, and random people from the audience kept dropping by and giving her dap, she had sent a call to action to all that heard her message.

"Yo', Diamond hit your girl up and said if I'm ever in Atlanta to hit her up and she got me." She told everybody in the section, and then she checked the number in her phone again to make sure it didn't erase or nothing.

"Ayye, hell I might need to head down there to Atlanta with you for real tho." Quan whispered to Cali anticipating that he might have to dip outta town and lay low for a while until things die down a bit after popping Moochie. "Bet," Cali replied with a smile and shook hands with

Quan to solidify their new partnership. Brooklyn told Ledarius that she had a surprise for him when they left tonight, and whispered in his ear that her mom was gone for the night and that meant that she had the house to herself.

Alikah and AK were hugged up together and making plans of their own. "Ayyye," everybody screamed when Miss Freeman showed up. "You know I ain't finna miss my babies out here becoming big stars and what not." Miss Freeman said still giving everyone hugs. Cali was a star, and she had her moment, and now she could carry on her brothers dream that he never got a chance to accomplish himself.

AK told Cali earlier about the symbolic significance of the number seven and its multiples such as the esoteric science of the angel number fourteen, which was the date of tonight's performance. Cali's light shined bright, and everybody captured it on their cell phones and shared it, which increased its chances of going viral.

"Look Cali," Camisha said as she showed her how many people and influencers were talking and reposting her performance, even Diamond had noticed and signaled for Cali to make sure she hit her up as they got ready to leave.

As they all gathered up their things to leave the club everybody was coming over for their last chance to network. AK and Alikah, Ledarius and Brooklyn and Fang and Vanessa and Maine and Psyke and the twins along with Cali and Dajon and Quan and Stimey and Snacks and Jacob all got up and headed out the door. These are the kids that society throws away when fathers, brothers, uncles and cousins get taken away due too soon, due to violence and incarceration.

On their way out of the club, Tick jumped in front of everybody and held up his phone. "Yo', I just thought about something." Tick said with the excitement of someone who knew something that everybody else didn't. "That last fight between you two," he quickly pointed to AK and Ledarius. "Never got uploaded, remember?" We all ran over there to Marcus when we heard the gun shots." Ledarius and AK looked at each other. "Y'all want me to hit send? Ye or Nay?" They looked at each other again and then looked back at Tick and said at the same time, "Ye" they both said simultaneously.

The video of the fight between AK and Ledarius was uploaded to the internet as they all left the club with Ledarius and Brooklyn hugged up together with AK and Alikah, hugged up right next to them and the rest of the gang right behind them.

A week later, on the same night that Ledarius took his oath into the Brotherhood of Assassins, Brooklyn had just finished reading, The Coldest Winter Ever by Sister Souljah. She still couldn't believe he just walked past her sitting in the car like that. She shook her head, afterwards she Googled Sister Souljah and looked through all the books she had written from *No Disrespect* on up. She scrolled past a news feed on her Facebook that said that a Chicago boy had rode down to Memphis and in a fit a jealous rage and shot his baby mother's new boyfriend and was now on the run from authorities. Brooklyn put her phone down and fired up her laptop, she was ready to begin writing her first novel. She went to Google Docs and wrote out the title.

"My Crazy Summer"

Written By

Brooklyn Carter

Then she wondered if Jay-Z and Beyonce had a book publishing company, because she felt like if she was going to spend all that time writing a whole entire book then she wanted it to be published by somebody that she admired. Her Google search turned up negative, but she had not given up hope, because the way that they be coming up with new business ventures. Maybe by the time she was finished they would have one or even maybe a film company to produce the movie. She daydreamed for little bit longer and then she got to work.

The End

Disclaimer:

Certain aspects of this book have been altered to maintain the integrity of the theatrical release.

Author contact

thenextdragonbook@gmail.com

IG: @thenextdragonbook